Alfred Lys Baldry

Sir John Everett Millais

His Art and Influence

Alfred Lys Baldry

Sir John Everett Millais
His Art and Influence

ISBN/EAN: 9783337399153

Printed in Europe, USA, Canada, Australia, Japan

Cover: Foto ©Raphael Reischuk / pixelio.de

More available books at **www.hansebooks.com**

Sir John Everett Millais

His Art and Influence

By A. L. Baldry

Author of " Albert Moore : His Life and Works,"
Etc.

LONDON
GEORGE BELL & SONS
1899

PREFACE

THERE is no intention to give in these pages anything approaching a detailed personal history of Sir John Millais, or to treat at any length the facts of his private life. Such matters are better left to the biographers who deal with the man and desire to draw a portrait of him as he lived. What is offered here is an appreciation of his influence upon the art of his time, an estimate of the value of his intervention, as an artist, in the æsthetic movements that marked the years over which his career extended. Therefore only those personal details have been included which are important because they have some bearing upon his professional progress, or have helped to confirm him in a preference for a particular line of action.

In the case of Sir John Millais this separation of the artist from the man is the easier, because, admirable and sincere though he was in his devotion to his profession, he did not make it his sole interest; but, outside his studio, threw himself into the occupations and amusements that are dear to every man of robust vitality, and are expressive of physical inclinations rather than intellectual gifts. Our concern is with him as a worker, as one of the greatest painters that the British School has known; and it is only incidentally necessary to refer to his domestic affairs when they happen to explain significantly how far his private pursuits aided in keeping up the splendid virility of his art. His pictures and drawings are the essential facts that have called for consideration, because by them his place in history is fixed; and as a commentary on them this book must be read.

Fortunately it has been possible, by the courtesy of the owners of the copyrights of his pictures, to summarise pictorially the many phases of his practice at the various stages of his working life, and to hint, as far as may be done with reproductions in black-and-white, at the greatness of his artistic ability. All sides of his art are illustrated, and the evidence given of his versatility is comprehensive and intelligible.

Sincere acknowledgment of very valuable assistance in the preparation of the letterpress is due to Mr M. H. Spielmann, who has also allowed the use of his exhaustive list of the artist's pictures, which was compiled originally for his book, " Millais and his Works"; and to Mr George Allen, by whose permission appear certain quotations from the writings of Mr Ruskin which have a particular reference to the performance of Sir John Millais.

CONTENTS

TITLE VIGNETTE TO
WORDSWORTH'S POEMS

LIST OF ILLUSTRATIONS

ix

LIST OF ILLUSTRATIONS

BOOKPLATE DESIGNED FOR
CHRISTOPHER SYKES

From a Picture by
Frank Holl   SIR J. E. MILLAIS, BART., P.R.A.

JOHN EVERETT MILLAIS

CHAPTER I

INTRODUCTORY

THE record of the British School of painting during the present century has been especially remarkable for its variety of incident. A curious series of episodes has very definitely affected the character of our national art practice, and has powerfully influenced the whole course of artistic progress. Events of the utmost moment have been numerous enough to make this period of our art history peculiarly significant as a time of active development, and to mark emphatically that growth of popular interest in aesthetic questions which is now bearing ample fruit. In all sorts of ways circumstances have combined to produce effects of extreme value, not only to art workers, but to every thinker as well, who wishes to arrive at a correct estimate of the manner in which taste controls the workings of our social economy.

Perhaps the most instructive feature of this century of development has been its extraordinary freedom from anything like ordered regularity. The aesthetic creed which is to-day so devoutly and so generally accepted has been formulated not on any careful and exact system, but rather as a result of occurrences apparently accidental. It has grown by slow stages and with many fluctuations, alternating between almost feverish impulse and absolute stagnation. Every now and then some happy chance has stimulated sudden movement, and caused a great advance; and then there has succeeded an equally marked retro-

A

gression, in which positions that appeared to be securely occupied were abandoned with unaccountable haste, and principles seemingly immutable were given up without even a momentary hesitation. A vigorous conflict of opinion has been in progress for the greater part of the time, and each phase of thought has in turn been accepted as an infallible revelation, calculated to settle finally and for ever all the points at issue.

What has at last come out of this prolonged strife is a reasonably definite agreement on main questions, a healthy acknowledgment of the right of all sides to a hearing, if only there is sincerity in what they have to say. The many-sidedness of art is admitted willingly enough; and a broad toleration of genuine effort encourages workers of the better sort to strive for the expression of their true convictions, secure in the belief that they will not be hastily misjudged. There is no longer any need for them to subject themselves to traditions which originated, not in an intelligent understanding of the facts upon which all sound aestheticism is based, but rather in a false idea of being in the fashion; they can choose their own manner of stating what they believe, and can use each his particular individuality to give variety and active vitality to their methods of practice.

It is quite worth while making some examination of the sequence of the events which have led to this emancipation. There is something to be learned by studying the apparent incoherences of thought and the obvious inconsistencies of performance characteristic of what has been the busiest period of our art history. When the century began, the influence of a group of great masters was still powerful to control the effort of their successors. Reynolds, Gainsborough, and Romney, had died only a few years before, but Laurence, Hoppner, Raeburn, Morland, and some other painters of scarcely less capacity, were carrying on the teaching of these chiefs of the British School; and

Turner was making the first manifestations of that extraordinary genius which in his maturer years was destined
to put beyond question his right to a place among the
greatest artists of the world. During the first decade,
Constable, De Wint, Wilkie, David Cox, Crome, and Etty,
came into the arena, to prove that the vitality of our
native art was still unimpaired, and that splendid achievement was possible to the workers who were able to
appreciate the intentions of their predecessors.

But as these men dropped one by one out of the ranks,
they left vacant places which no one was competent to fill,
and before the middle of the century was reached a painful
change had come about in the condition of affairs. The
purity and vigour of the aesthetic belief by which the
masters had been guided had given way to a lamentable
love of trivialities, to a worship of an artificial style, and to
a preference for pedantic methods. Weak conventions,
based upon absolute misconceptions, perverted the whole
range of artistic production, and parodied the principles
which had proved before supremely fitted to encourage
nobility of intention and strength of practice. The smooth
and careful commonplaces of Mulready, the feeble pretti-
nesses of Augustus Egg, the bombast of P. F. Poole, the
theatrical exaggeration of C. R. Leslie, the pretentious
affectation of Maclise, and the skilful but uninspired
mechanism of Landseer, misled the public taste, and
warped even the professional judgment. An extraordinary degeneration set in, a helpless surrender of all
the conquests by which our school had been so recently
enriched. Strange gods were worshipped, a curious faith
in false creeds became the fashion, and fanaticism without
logic or reason was substituted for intelligent analysis
and accurate judgment.

The causes of this degeneration must be sought in something beyond the mere incapacity of the workers themselves at this particular period. It cannot be accounted
for simply by the failure of a whole group of men to reach

the standard of executive perfection to which their predecessors had easily attained; nor can it be put down only
to a freak of nature who had endowed the artists of one
century less generously than those who had lived in the
one immediately preceding. What had really happened
was a change of thought, a complete upset of the convictions by which the art of this country had hitherto been
controlled. Reynolds, Gainsborough, and their contemporaries and immediate followers, were close students of
reality, and, with all their love of style, never sacrificed
truth to effective artifice. They had a sound instinct for
splendour of technical method, and understood perfectly
what devices of execution would give to their work an
impressive dignity, and a persuasive refinement. Their
pictures combined rich harmony of colour relation, strength
of design, and certainty of statement, to an exceptional
degree; but were always based securely upon nature and
owed to earnest regard for her direction their superlative
quality of easy mastery. Sincerity and absence of affectation made them valuable as object-lessons in executive
management, and surrounded them with that atmosphere
of robust vitality which is rightly accepted as the hall-
mark of excellence.

Yet the value of these examples of perfectly controlled
aestheticism was so little appreciated by the men who
were responsible for the art production of the middle years
of the century that the introduction of a debased and
senseless form of practice became possible. The artists
who might have carried on the noblest traditions of our
school, and might, even with their limitations of technical
skill, have done credit to themselves and their surroundings,
preferred to substitute feeble and inanimate theories for
the honest beliefs which were presented for their adoption.
They blinded themselves with fallacies about the merits of
a style founded not upon exact observation of nature but
upon abstractions that they were pleased to consider

intellectual and imaginative.   It was, they thought, a sign
of weakness to study the facts of the world about them or
to show that they had either the capacity or the inclination
to deal with realities.   Their duty was to trust their own
inspirations, and to make up by readiness of invention for
their deficiency of visual training.   The farther they got
away from the taint of naturalism the better they were
pleased, for the more completely did they believe that they
were fulfilling their mission.

With such a view of their responsibilities it was not
surprising that year by year they should have sunk
deeper into the slough of convention.   They had no
guide but their own erring fancy, no control but that of
fashion, and were merely drifting helplessly in whatever
direction the delusions of the moment might lead them.
Naturally their art degenerated and dwindled, until it
was on the verge of extinction.   A little honesty of
purpose might have saved it; a touch of sturdy self-
respect might have awakened it to a sense of its futile
incompetence; but instead it preferred to continue in its
foolish courses, glorying in its disabilities, and unconscious,
or careless, of the fate that was awaiting it in the near
future.

To put matters once again on a proper footing very
drastic measures were necessary.   There was nothing to
be gained by compromises, or by dealing gently with the
misconceptions which were hurrying the British school to
extinction.   The only possible cure for the ills with which
it was at this time afflicted was a radical change of policy
forcibly imposed upon the artists themselves, and upon the
people whom they were misleading.   Clearly the decline of
professional taste had gone so far that no remedies which
affected details merely could be expected to prove
beneficial.   Only an absolute abandonment of the false
principles which were responsible for the degeneration,
and a sustained effort to begin again with due humility

and real sincerity, could ensure anything like a hope
prospect for the future. A new direction had to be fou
for aesthetic endeavour, and a different basis upon whi
to build up a scheme of practice. The delusions abc
intellectual art, the blind worship of unmeaning sty
and empty abstractions, all the fallacious absurdities whi
had encouraged the descent from the sublime to t
ridiculous that had been in progress, had to be destroy
without mercy. Vehement and unhesitating oppositi
to the prevailing fashion was all that could be depend
upon to effectually alter the course of affairs, and
awaken the art world sufficiently to a sense of
position to give a proper trial to the more wholesor
methods which were needed to replace those that we
plainly discredited and obsolete.

What had to come was a return to the studious natur
ism that was as surely the attribute of the work of t
eighteenth-century British masters as it has been t
supreme merit of the great canvases by masters of oth
schools. As anything like recantation was not to
expected on the part of the men who in the wisdc
of their own conceit had been setting up their we
opinions against the commanding authority of the lead
of the profession, there was little hope that a belated cc
version would make them active in any attempt at refor
The change had to be brought about without their he
and it involved ousting them from a position to whi
they were not entitled. Happily the means of doi
this proved at the critical moment to be available, mea
most effective, and exactly calculated to produce resu
that were not only beneficial, but also permanent.

Opportunely enough, when matters were at their wor
and our art was seemingly at its lowest ebb, a grow
of young artists suddenly raised the standard of rev
against the inefficiency of their elders, and asserted wi
all the courage of youth their disbelief in the creed th

they found themselves called upon to accept. They came forward to challenge the advocates of the existing state of art politics and to wage war against what they felt to be pernicious and unnatural doctrines. The suddenness of the onslaught made it necessarily all the more dramatic. There was a degree of unexpectedness about this declaration of a new opinion that drew upon it more immediate attention than it might otherwise have gained, and gave it a surprising power to excite the keenest possible interest. Of course, the interest took the form of bitter opposition in a great many cases, and the young reformers found themselves committed to a very strenuous conflict, but they had the resolution to persevere, and to meet attack with redoubled assertion.

It was not long before allies began to gather round them. Their enthusiasm proved to be contagious, and their tenacity excited first wonder and then respect. People seemed to realise that perhaps there was something worth considering in a movement which was supported with so much confidence, and that ideas advanced with such evident conviction were not to be lightly dismissed as the fancies of eccentric innovators. A few of the better type of thinkers on art subjects joined themselves to the rebels, and with a sincere acknowledgment of the justice of their cause, gave them effective and practical encouragement as well as intelligent advocacy. Slowly, but surely, a consciousness of the inadequacy of the existing conventions spread in many directions, and step by step a healthier and saner phase of belief won its way to general acceptance. Doubts as to the infallibility of the professors of theories that were proclaimed to be false and mistaken increased, until the whole array of delusions that had been gathered together was scattered before the irresistible advance of the forces of enlightened common-sense. That the only inspiration by which the artist can profit must come from nature, and that the purer this inspiration is kept the better the results it will give, was in a little while frankly recognised; and with this recognition came not only a complete reform of professional practice, but also a marked improvement in the popular capacity to sympathise with artistic effort.

At first the party of progress, as was to be expected from the nature of the task they had undertaken, was not prepared to abate one atom of their assertion of the principles to which they had pinned their faith. They had an obstinate fanaticism to upset, and to do this they had to profess a stronger obstinacy and a fanaticism more uncompromising. Their view was definite to the verge of brutality, and was stated with a directness that left no opening for quibbles about their meaning. Naturalism was the corner-stone of their creed, so they would tolerate nothing in art which did not reproduce nature with scrupulous fidelity and minute exactness. Every little detail, every small accessory, must be carefully and lovingly studied from actual objects, and no part of the subject selected might be slurred over or disregarded as a trivial or unimportant thing. A perfect whole could only be built up by absolute perfection in every one of its components, for nature's severe completeness was held to be simply a result of her infinite complexity.

So, to justify their attack upon the men who rejected nature as something common and unclean, an associate unfit for the companionship of imaginative and inventive minds, these young artists put themselves with a kind of child-like trust utterly and entirely into her hands, and paraded their dependence upon her for the world to see. Had they been less convinced, or less sure of the position they had taken up, their influence would scarcely have been strong enough to over-ride an established fashion. Their only hope lay in so defining the contrast between what they preached and practised, and what was advocated by the rest of the profession, that there could be no doubt

LOVE

about the reality of their belief. They had determined on a protest, and, with sound judgment, they took care that they did not weaken its effect by any failure to make their essential points with absolute clearness.

But when once the principle for which they were fighting had gained acceptance, and the need for their intervention was gratefully recognised, they did not hesitate to modify the extreme rigour of their manner. They and their followers—for it was not long before other young artists began to join them—found other ways of interpreting nature without toiling to reproduce all her infinite variety in each closely detailed and elaborately realised picture. They proved that exquisite accuracy was possible with less technical restraint, and less labour to be simply imitative. The larger facts that she presents to the earnest student, could be used pictorially with just as much truth, and just as much honesty, as the little things which call for patience rather than largeness of vision; and a less deliberate method of execution could be made to express quite as many meanings as the precise and careful brushwork which records every vein on a leaf or every feather in a bird's wing.

As the purely militant side of the movement ceased to call for emphasis, its wider artistic possibilities came more clearly to the front; and, though the craving for naturalism has remained ever since as the source of all that is best in the modern art production, the chances open to the workers who have built their practice upon the ground won for them in the middle of the century are still increasing year by year.

In one sense, the astonishing revival of aesthetic intelligence which has made itself evident during recent times is accidental, in that it is to be ascribed simply to the fortunate appearance, at the right moment, of certain men with sufficient strength of character to stem a seemingly irresistible tide of degeneration. But in

another, it is the direct outcome of effort
public taste, and to foster a truer understandi
questions. When the battle of the new sc
the old was won, there was nothing to c
unlimited development, for there was no
barrier of narrow and irrational conventions
way to better things. A wider scope brouչ
type of achievement and a sounder appreci
relative importance of those devices by whiⅽ
tions of the artist can be made credible. A
sional and public point of view expanded, ⅼ
distinguish between good traditions and ba⸱
efficient, and the inclination to produce ar.
work of permanent value gained a greater ⅼ

Sincerity, and an honest desire to profit by
of nature, have come at last to be recog
essentials for success in art; and if the workⲉ
satisfactorily that from first to last they are in
devotion to these principles, they have no ⲅ
that their individuality will not be respected.
personal interpretation of the facts by wh
impressed will be denied consideration. Liber
and, if they satisfy the one fundamental condit
freedom of action, are gladly allowed to th
hint of a return to the worship of formal pⲅ
or any show of liking for trivial affectations, ⸱
tolerated. The condition of affairs at thⲉ
century repeats, only on a larger scale, that ⱱ
at the beginning; and the fallacies that haⱱ
between these two epochs of masterly ⸱
happily ceased to be anything but an unpleaⲋ
Healthy vitality has taken the place of mⲟ
tude; and in its restored and robust strengⲧ
school is capable once again of holding its
any competitors it. may chance to meet.

Concerning the men themselves, who weⲓ

sponsible for this awakening of the better instincts of the art community, there is something to be said. They stand out as conspicuous figures in our history, prominent as much on account of their rare gifts and capacities, as by reason of their courage and perseverance in asserting the principles to which they had pinned their faith. If they had not been endowed with more than ordinary qualifications for their work in life, they could scarcely have made their propagandism so effective; while without the most assured confidence in the justice of their cause they could not have kept their enthusiasm alive through the long struggle that they had to face before they could feel themselves certain of victory. But, fortunately, they summarised between them all that was necessary to arrest and retain the attention of everyone who had any real receptivity and any inclination to examine the inner meaning of artistic practice. As a group they combined peculiar accuracy of vision, infinite fertility of imagination, true originality of method and manner, and a sturdy self-reliance and tenacity that could be depended upon in any emergency. They were bound together by a strong tie of sympathy, by a perfect understanding of their mutual aims, and by a common instinct to reject everything that seemed to them to be antagonistic to the purity of art.

That they influenced one another at first can scarcely be doubted; it was natural that their association for a particular end, and their isolation from the rest of the painting fraternity, should have brought them into a somewhat close agreement on details of procedure. But this influence by no means extended into a control of their personal views, and plainly it did not swamp their distinctive individualities. Indeed, as a demonstration of the wide applicability of a consistent creed, the variety of their work had a very definite persuasiveness, for it was well adapted to convince the sincere student that a respect for sound principles did not imply any sacrifice of personal liberty, or any surrender of the right to independent thought.

The chief figures in the group, the leaders round whom, as time went on, gathered a host of followers, were Ford Madox Brown, Dante Gabriel Rossetti, Holman Hunt, and John Everett Millais ; and certainly it would be hard to find a quartette offering fuller opportunity for interesting comparisons. Each member of it is to be credited with the possession of some special qualities that distinguished him from the others. Ford Madox Brown, for instance, was a man of infinite industry, a curiously earnest thinker, whose respect for fact led him to minutely realise the most intimate details of the life he selected to illustrate, and a lover of quaint symbolism with an extremely acute sense of the dramatic value of the little touches by which he filled up his pictorial narratives. Rossetti was steeped in poetic fancy, an exponent of everything recondite and fanciful, and the slave of an imagination which knew no limitations ; and was subject to none of the laws of logic. He lacked nothing of sincerity in his worship of nature ; but she was to him rather the source of suggestions that he enjoyed adapting than an absolute model whom he wished to represent with imitative exactness. Holman Hunt was, and is, a painter with a well-defined religious tendency that has not only governed his choice of subject, but has also given to his art a peculiar earnestness and devout intention. No influence has at any period of his life been able to turn him from the direction he chose in his youth, and he paints now, as he did then, with unquestioning conviction.

It is possible that if the success of the campaign against the old fallacies had depended solely upon the exertions and example of these three artists, it might have been far less immediate and convincing. Untiring industry, endless imagination, and the most devout conscience would

have had, beyond doubt, a real power of appeal to certain
classes of thinkers; and there would have been many
people ready and willing to attach themselves to men
who showed the highest development of these particular
attributes; but what would have resulted would have been
rather the forming of detached sects, each acknowledging
the authority of a single head, than the stimulating into
permanent activity of a great movement susceptible of
unlimited expansion, and based upon immutable principles.
What was needed to unite these diverse individualities,
and to bring into existence a combination of forces so
thorough and coherent that it would solidly sway the
whole mass of public opinion, was the co-operation of a
robust fighter, able to dominate by his personal authority
all the rest of his associates, and with an endowment of
qualities varied and brilliant enough to gain the popular
attention as a matter of course. Such an one was fortunately available in the person of John Everett Millais;
and to him may fairly be given the chief credit for the
final triumph of the cause which more than anyone else
he strove to keep alive.
    Indeed, it is not too much to say that the awakening of
British art, of which we are enjoying the fruits to-day,
owes to him the greater part of its completeness. That he
was admirably supported by the men who were one with
him in aesthetic intention is not to be denied; and that
he would have been unable alone, and without active
sympathisers as tenacious as himself, to convert the whole
community to saner beliefs is, if the limitations of human
energy are considered, more than likely. But if he had
not been in the front of the battle the victory would have
been a hollow one, and its effects would have been only
partial. He was the one commanding figure who could
engage the attention of the widest circle of art-lovers, and
by the attractiveness of his personality put himself on
good terms even with his opponents. Nothing was too

difficult for him to attack, no obstacle seemed to him insurmountable, and there was no test of his courage that he was unwilling to undergo. Through everything he kept up the same determined spirit, undaunted by opposition and unspoiled by success, carrying with him the men whose natures were less adapted for the active assertion of a logical artistic policy, and, finally, by the weight of his own cheerful belief in the significance of his mission, conquering all the forces of indifference and spiteful self-interest which had been arrayed against him by the supporters of the old order of things.

To understand the extent of his influence, it is necessary to analyse his personality, and to examine those details of his character which had the chief share in shaping his destiny. His nature was not a complex one, and was free from the curious contradictions which often defy explanation. No want of agreement between the habits of his daily existence and the manner of his art made him incomprehensible, or suggested any doubt of his sincerity. On the contrary, the direct and straightforward honesty, the sturdy independence, and the masculine vigour, which were the guiding principles of his life, were also the causes by which the particular trend of his aesthetic convictions was determined. He put his real self into his art, and its manly simplicity was the result of his habitual unwillingness to confuse himself with side issues, or to stray into speculations which, for all their fascination, gave no plain promise of success. As a matter of fact, his imagination was not of the type that feeds on abstractions, and he had not the sort of mind which enjoys playing with dreams and fancies rather than facts.

The redundancy of thought which shows in everything that Rossetti produced, and marks him as an inventive genius with an almost uncontrollable craving for imagery and symbolical suggestion, can hardly be said to have

been ever a possibility in the case of Millais. He had no instinct for contemplative habits, and no inclination to yield to that custom of introspection by which morbid preferences are only too apt to be encouraged. Yet he had poetry in him, but poetry of a kind that comes from a love of Nature, and from the constant and devoted study of her charms. He could feel the attraction of a piece of exquisite scenery, and he was entirely responsive to the witchery of a dainty personality; but he hardly ever tried to build upon what he felt a strange edifice of wild devices with peculiar cryptic significations. It was sufficient for him to record the beauty that he enjoyed; and he was satisfied if he could give to other people, by his rendering, something of the pleasure that the exercise of his faculty of observation had brought to him.

In his youth, when he was closely associated with men like Rossetti and Holman Hunt, he showed himself, it is true, to be so far in sympathy with their aspirations that he met them not only on the common ground of naturalism, but as well on that of symbolism. His earlier pictures, such canvases as "Christ in the House of His Parents," "Ferdinand lured by Ariel," "Mariana in the Moated Grange," and "The Woodman's Daughter," for example, were not wanting in touches designed to amplify the pictorial story, embroideries on the main motive, which, by their variety, made the whole meaning more attractive, and provided a series of little by-plots to support and explain the dramatic purpose of the work.

When, however, the necessity for this intimate association diminished, as the condition of art politics improved, and the rout of the old conventions became indisputable, he gave himself up more and more to the avowal of his independent conviction. He ceased to exert himself to weave curious webs of fancy, preferring instead to use his amazing technical power to realise the pleasanter aspects of Nature. Gradually, but surely, his manner changed, passing through the phase of quieter and less elaborated imagination, which was best illustrated by " The Random Shot," " Autumn Leaves," " Apple Blossoms," and " The Vale of Rest," until, at last, in the middle of his life, came the sudden development of that convincing certainty of selection and practice, by which the real greatness of his ability was impressed upon the public mind.

In this he was following the course that his instincts taught him to prefer. While the fervour of protest was upon him, and the vigour of his antagonism to dogmas that he disliked swayed his judgment, he tried sincerely enough to adapt his methods to those of the men who were on his side in the struggle, and he strengthened his influence over them by concessions to their inclinations, and by giving practical proof of his interest in their aims. But when he felt that he had the chance to extend his authority beyond the limits of a purely professional agitation, and to touch a larger public than would have been within his reach if he had continued only to advocate the extreme views that agreed well enough with his early enthusiasm, he very wisely did not waste his opportunity. By minor modifications that involved no surrender of the essential articles of his creed, he made his art perfectly comprehensible, gathering thereby a whole host of supporters, and, by his consideration for the general taste, establishing his popularity, and that of the school he represented, permanently and effectively.

With all his discretion, and all his keen understanding of the tactics needed-for carrying to success a piece of complicated policy, he would certainly not have had so great a personal influence if his artistic qualifications had been less indisputable. Even when he was most attacked, at the time when all that ridicule could do to kill the movement that he was fighting to encourage was being

AUTUMN LEAVES

tried by artists and critics alike, no one was bold enough to deny that he was endowed by nature with extraordinary gifts. He was accused freely enough of want of judgment, deliberate eccentricity, wilful disregard of aesthetic proprieties, irreverence, obstinacy, and a whole host of other evil tendencies, but never of incapacity. In fact, the consciousness of his amazing strength was the inspiring cause of the bitterness with which his early work was received; and when, after a while, angry disparagement and ridicule both died away in a kind of sulky despair, it was this same sense of his power that led lovers of art to accept him as a leader whose authority was not to be questioned.

Perhaps the most eloquent and acute estimate of the personal fitness of Millais for the profession he followed, and the best statement of his claim to rank among the chief men of our school, came from Mr Ruskin, whose earnest recognition of the purity of the motives by which the whole band of young reformers was actuated was one of the first and greatest pieces of encouragement that the movement received. He, at least, took them seriously, and felt with them the necessity for strenuous opposition to those blind guides of a blind public whose unfitness for any educational work he clearly perceived. In Millais he most plainly discovered the qualities that make for mighty achievement, and in a passage in one of his books he draws a parallel between him and that other giant in British art, J. M. W. Turner, that in its exquisite appreciation is unsurpassable. So significant, indeed, it is, that it may, without apology, be quoted at length as an exact word-picture, recording with absolute accuracy every intimate feature of his artistic personality.

" It is always to be remembered," the great critic writes, " that no one mind is like another, either in its powers or perceptions; and while the main principles of training must be the same for all, the result in each will be as various as the kinds of truth which each will apprehend;

B

therefore, also, the modes of effort, even in men whose inner principles and final aims are exactly the same. Suppose, for instance, two men, equally honest, equally industrious, equally impressed with a humble desire to render some part of what they saw in nature faithfully; and, otherwise, trained in convictions such as I have endeavoured to induce. But one of them is quiet in temperament, has a feeble memory, no invention, and excessively keen sight. The other is impatient in temperament, has a memory which nothing escapes, an invention which never rests, and is comparatively near-sighted.

"Set them both free in the same field in a mountain valley. One sees everything, small and large, with almost the same clearness; mountains and grasshoppers alike; the leaves on the branches, the veins in the pebbles, the bubbles in the stream; but he can remember nothing, and invent nothing. Patiently he sets himself to his mighty task; abandoning at once all thoughts of seizing transient effects, or giving general impressions of that which his eyes present to him in microscopical dissection, he chooses some small portion out of the infinite scene, and calculates with courage the number of weeks which must elapse before he can do justice to the intensity of his perceptions, or the fulness of matter in his subject.

"Meantime, the other has been watching the change of the clouds and the march of the light along the mountain sides; he beholds the entire scene in broad, soft masses of true gradation, and the very feebleness of his sight is in some sort an advantage to him, in making him more sensible of the aërial mystery of distance, and hiding from him the multitudes of circumstances which it would have been impossible for him to represent. But there is not one change in the casting of the jagged shadows along the hollows of the hills, but it is fixed on his mind for ever; not a flake of spray has broken from the sea of

THE ORDER OF RELEASE

cloud about their bases, but he has watched it as it melts away, and could recall it to its lost place in heaven by the slightest effort of his thoughts. Not only so, but thousands and thousands of such images, of older scenes, remain congregated in his mind, each mingling in new associations with those now visibly passing before him, and these again confused with other images of his own ceaseless, sleepless imagination, flashing by in sudden troops. Fancy how his paper will be covered with stray symbols and blots, and undecipherable shorthand :—as for his sitting down to 'draw from nature' there was not one of the things which he wished to represent, that stayed for so much as five seconds together : but none of them escaped for all that : they are sealed up in that strange storehouse of his ; he may take one of them out perhaps, this day twenty years, and paint it in his dark room, far away. Now, observe, you may tell both of these men, when they are young, that they are to be honest, that they have an important function, and that they are not to care what Raphael did. This you may wholesomely impress on them both. But fancy the exquisite absurdity of ex- pecting either of them to possess any of the qualities of the other.

" I have supposed the feebleness of sight in the last, and of invention in the first painter, that the contrast between them might be more striking ; but, with very slight modification, both the characters are real. Grant to the first considerable inventive power, with exquisite sense of colour ; and give to the second, in addition to all his other faculties, the eye of an eagle ; and the first is John Everett Millais, the second Joseph Mallard William Turner."

This exhaustive consideration of Millais as an artist, written though it was in the earlier years of his career, before his opinions had settled into mature stability, is equally applicable to the work of his whole life. It expresses exactly the manner of his instinctive preferences, and clearly defines the sources of his controlling influence upon our native art. He saw things as most people wish to see them, with absolute clearness of vision, and stated them frankly and sturdily without any effort to impose a peculiar view of his own upon the rest of the world. Realism was always the one unalterable fact by which he was guided, and the changes which, in the course of time, came in his purely technical methods, never affected the intention that inspired his whole range of achievement. It is as strongly perceptible in " The North-West Passage," as in " The Order of Release " or " The Minuet"; it governs the treatment of the " Yeoman of the Guard," as surely as that of " Ophelia," or " The Huguenot"; and it gives to his portrait of Mr Gladstone, painted in 1885, the same vivid actuality that distinguished the " Portrait of a Gentleman and his Grandchild " produced as far back as 1849.

To the last his art remained completely convinced; and it never lost its power over other minds than his. The many capable men who sprang up around him, pledged to the principles which he was advocating, never diminished his popularity by attracting to themselves any part of his following.   No competition was powerful enough to oust him from his pre-eminence ; and he retained to his death the fruits of the victory he won in his youth.   His place in the history of the century is an assured one ; he gained it fairly, and he held it by sheer strength of individuality and by the obvious superiority of his artistic qualities.

#1

• Sir John Everett Millais; His Art +
Influences by A.L. Baldry.
London: George Bell + Sons. 1899

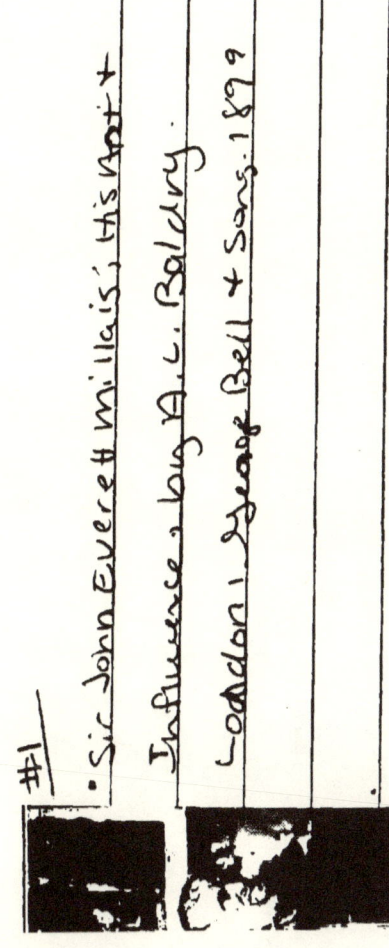

CHAPTER II

IT was apparently to his ancestry that the artist who has played so important a part in the resuscitation of British art owed his spirit and his energy in attacking established institutions. He came of a stock which was, in bygone centuries, by no means unready for conflict with people in authority. The family, of Norman origin, settled in Jersey at some date anterior to the Conquest, and it held for nearly seven hundred years a position of some prominence among the land-holders of that island. Many entries in the local records tend to imply that the members of the Millais clan were men of importance, powerful enough to set themselves in opposition to their over-lords, and to the ecclesiastical officials, who tried to exact from them dues and acknowledgments that they were unwilling to render, and the recurrence of these entries is frequent enough to suggest that this independence was something more than occasional.

The estates they held seem to have varied in different generations, or else there were branches of the family in many parts of the island, for at various times the name, in one or other of its many forms, appears in the documents of most of the parishes. In 1331 Geoffray Milayes is entered in the Royal Rent Roll; in 1381 John and Guille Millais are recorded as paying taxes to the Prior of St Clement's; in the middle of the fifteenth century the head of the family, who usually was named John, settled in the parish of St Saviour; and in 1527 Clement Myllais, presumably one of his descendants, was

21

Rector of that parish. By the marriage, ab
John Myllais to the heiress of the Le Jardera
estate, in the parish of St Saviour, came int
and remained in their possession until the beg
present century; and in 1668 another Joh
mentioned as a tenant of the Crown in the
Grouville and St Clement. The name, even
served in the island; for there is a village call
in the parish of St Ouen, and a range of hills
east of St Heliers is known as " Les Monts M:

Although John Everett Millais was born
1829, at Portland Place, Southampton, his f:
inhabitant of Jersey, and an officer in the is
The first five years of the child's life were sp
but in 1835 he was taken by his parents '
Brittany, where he began, by his sketches of t
the place and the types of the people, to
convincing proofs of the remarkable artistic
was in him. These early efforts were so su
attracted so much attention outside his famil
when he was not more than nine years
brought to London for an expert opinion on
in the profession for which he seemed pre-de:
President of the Royal Academy, Sir Martin .
was consulted, and his encouraging decl:
" Nature had provided for the boy's success,'
future of the young artist, who was at once
begin serious study. In 1838 he entered t
school in Bloomsbury which was carried o
Sass, and regarded. as the best available p
training of budding genius. In the same yea:
silver medal of the Society of Arts, for a draw
antique, and caused quite a sensation when
at the distribution of the prizes, to receive his
the Duke of Sussex, who was presiding. Th
the spectators is said to have been unbounde

Millais" came forward, a tiny child in a pinafore, to answer to his name, and even the officials at first found it hard to believe that he would be really the winner of the medal.

For two years he remained under the tuition of Mr Sass, an artist who during the earlier years of this century exhibited at the Royal Academy and other exhibitions a great many portraits and figure-pictures that are now forgotten. He deserves to be remembered, not on account of his own success as a painter, but because he gave to many men who have since become famous their first grounding in artistic knowledge. With his teaching, and a good deal of work from the casts in the British Museum, the boy developed so rapidly that when he was only eleven years old he gained admission to the Royal Academy Schools, the youngest student, it is said, that has ever been received into them. His career there was a series of successes. For six years he laboured indefatigably, and gave proof of his ability by taking prize after prize, beginning with a silver medal in 1843, and ending, in 1847, with the gold medal for a historical picture, "The Tribe of Benjamin seizing the Daughters of Shiloh."

Subjects of this type seem at that time to have attracted him strongly, and to have occupied a great deal of his attention, for in 1846 he had painted, and exhibited at the Academy, "Pizarro seizing the Inca of Peru," which is now in the South Kensington Museum, and in the following year another study of violent action, "Elgiva seized by Order of Archbishop Odo." To 1847 also belongs the great design, "The Widow bestowing her Mite," for the Westminster Hall competition, a canvas fourteen feet long by ten feet high, covered with life-size figures. Such an effort speaks well for the energy and ambition of a lad of eighteen, who could within the space of a few months carry out so vast an undertaking in addition to the "Elgiva," and his gold medal picture.

So far his progress had been, from the point of view of the older men, who were busy with their pompous artificialities, extremely satisfactory and promising. He had proved himself to be possessed of rare gifts, and he had begun to paint just the sort of bombast which was then entirely fashionable. To all appearance historical art was to have in him an exponent of exactly the type required to infuse into its dry bones some spark of vitality, and to give to its fallacious traditions a touch of credibility. But, happily for the art of the country, these expectations were doomed to disappointment. He had only been feeling his way, and, not having had time as yet to analyse his inclinations, he had temporarily accepted, with youthful imitativeness, the precepts of his teachers and fellow-students. It did not take him long to discover that he was on the wrong track, and to decide that there was in another direction a far better opportunity for the assertion of his own independent convictions. Indeed, he showed in the shaping of his artistic policy, and in the arranging of his methods of expression, the same precocity that had distinguished his manifestation of technical skill. Before he could have been expected to have come to any clear opinion about the relative advantage of different phases of thought, he had actually made up his mind that the school, of which, for the moment, circumstances had made him a member, was fundamentally wrong, and that his mission in life was to destroy it.

He was just nineteen when he elected to take upon himself this responsibility. About the middle of the year 1848, he, and his friends Rossetti and Holman Hunt, inspired partly by the example of Ford Madox Brown, and partly by their own study of the works of the Italian Primitives who, before the time of Raphael, had laboured with devout and simple naturalism, formed the idea of

THE HUGUENOT

·everting to a type of art which contained the germs of
great achievement. They decided, then and there, that
the principles which guided the early masters, and made
their productions so convincing, were being deliberately
ignored by the modern men, whose second-hand practices
were based upon the conventions created by a long line of
degenerate successors of Raphael and his contemporaries.
So these three youths agreed among themselves to break
away from the rules and regulations by which they had
been bound in their student days, and to proclaim the
truths that they felt their teachers had withheld from them.
From this agreement sprang into existence an association
that, despite the small number of its members and the
shortness of its life, has left upon the history of the British
School a mark clear and ineffaceable. ·*

The Pre-Raphaelite Brotherhood, as this association
was called by way of plainly declaring the intentions and
ambitions of the men who belonged to it, was formally
constituted during the autumn of 1848.   It included,
in addition to the three originators, two other painters,
James Collinson and F. G. Stephens, a sculptor, Thomas
Woolner, and a writer, William Michael Rossetti, who
acted as secretary of the Brotherhood.   Ford Madox
Brown never became a member, although he entirely sympathised with the artistic aims of the group, for he had,
it is said, doubts concerning the utility of such a banding
together, and was more inclined to favour independent
action ; but several other young painters, who were never
formally of the company, gave it practical support, and
openly adopted its methods. Indeed, the list of these
outside sympathisers soon became a long one ; it included
such able workers as William Bell Scott, Arthur Hughes,
Thomas Seddon, W. L. Windus, and W. H. Deverell, who
were directly inspired by the beliefs of the Brotherhood ;
and if, as would be quite legitimate, it were extended to
take in all the others whose first essays in art were

controlled by Pre-Raphaelite principles, an astonishing number of artists who have reached high rank in their profession could be added to it.

At first the inner significance of the Pre-Raphaelite movement was lost upon the general public. When, in 1849, Millais exhibited at the Academy his " Lorenzo and Isabella," by which his adoption of the new creed was plainly enough asserted, the picture was not unkindly received. It was ridiculed, perhaps, by the people who realised that it showed an artistic intention somewhat unlike that which was then generally prevalent; but its novelty of manner was put down to the youth and in-experience of the artist, and was regarded as a minor defect that a few more years of practice would remedy.

But in January 1850, the Brotherhood took a step that very effectually removed any doubts that were felt by the public about the meaning of such canvases. They began to issue a monthly magazine, called *The Germ*, in which they and their friends stated with sufficient plainness what Pre-Raphaelitism really meant, and what were the opinions that they professed. As a commercial speculation the magazine must be reckoned a failure, for after the fourth number it ceased to be issued, and at no time had it any general circulation. It served its purpose, however, of making quite intelligible the creed of its promoters ; and it gave to the world certain etchings of Holman Hunt, Collinson, Madox Brown, and Deverell, and much literary matter by Coventry Patmore, Woolner, W. B. Scott, F. G. Stephens, the two Rossettis and their sister Christina, and some other writers. An etching was prepared by Millais for the fifth number, an illustration of a story that Dante Rossetti was to write; but this fifth number did not appear.

Though *The Germ* died so quickly for want of sup port, it had fully accomplished what was required of i in the way of propagandism. When the next batch o Pre-Raphaelite efforts was exhibited in the spring of 1850

THE RETURN OF THE DOVE
TO THE ARK

there was no trace of hesitation or toleration in the comments of the older artists and the press. A perfect storm of abuse broke out. Against "Ferdinand lured by Ariel," and "Christ in the House of His Parents," which were the chief pictures sent by Millais to the Academy, the bitterest attack was directed. They were pronounced to be revolutionary and repulsive; and even their technical ability was misrepresented. Everything that could be said or done to minimise their influence, and to discredit the motives by which they were inspired, was lavished upon them without restraint, in a kind of frenzy of anguished excitement.

All this, however, was mild in comparison with the agitation in the following year, when it was seen that the Pre-Raphaelites, instead of bowing to the storm and recanting their opinions, were prepared to go to even greater lengths in the avowal of their convictions. The opposition had done its best to howl them down, and to frighten them by ferocious threats; but all this expenditure of misapplied energy had had no result. Millais exhibited "The Woodman's Daughter," "The Return of the Dove to the Ark," and "Mariana in the Moated Grange," and Holman Hunt "Valentine and Sylvia"; while the other members of the group gave equally definite proofs of their intention to persevere in the course they had adopted.

Alarm at this defiance, and perhaps an uneasy consciousness of the real strength of a movement that gave so little sign of yielding to pressure, drove the supporters of the existing condition of affairs to almost incredible lengths. They demanded that these canvases should be removed from the exhibition of the Academy, summarily expelled as outrages on good taste; they urged the students in the art schools to shun the Brotherhood, and everyone connected with it, as a source of infection, breeding plagues that, unless promptly stamped out, must inevitably destroy all that was best and purest in the art of the country;

they descended to the lowest depths of misrepresentation, and drew the line at nothing in the way of exaggeration. Calm and critical judgment ceased, for the moment, to exist, and a hysterical absence of balance threw into confusion even the best ordered and judicious minds.

This outburst had one immediate effect, an unpleasant one for the young artists, it checked for a while the sale of their pictures. "Christ in the House of His Parents," had been painted on commission for a well-known dealer, and it remained for many years on his hands; but "Ferdinand lured by Ariel," which had also been commissioned, was refused by the intending purchaser. It was afterwards sold to Mr Richard Ellison, a collector of rare discrimination, who was introduced to Millais by a mutual friend. Other canvases belonging to the same period either returned from the exhibitions to the artist's studio, or were parted with at low prices, and on terms of payment none too favourable.

But in a little while things began to mend. The virulence of the defenders of vested interests exhausted itself; and here and there strong men showed themselves ready to champion the cause of the Pre-Raphaelites. Mr Ruskin came into the arena, an enthusiastic advocate of an undertaking that was in every way calculated to appeal to his vivid sympathies. He criticised with no hesitating utterance the bitter fallacies of the self-constituted keepers of the public conscience; he met attack with counter-attack; and he declared with acute and prophetic insight that the pilloried artists were laying "the foundations of a school of art nobler than the world has seen for three hundred years." His explanations of their methods, and defence of their view of nature, were just what were needed to set people thinking, and to undermine the popularity of the dogmatic preachers of. false doctrines. Some years, it is true, elapsed before his enthusiasm, and the dogged perseverance of the young

APPLE BLOSSOMS

men, finally converted the great majority of art lovers, but the conversion did come, and it was complete.

Meanwhile Millais was manfully playing his part in the struggle, giving no sign that he minded being, as he put it in after years, "so dreadfully bullied." Nothing could shake his resolve to work out his artistic destiny in the way he thought best, and opposition only strengthened his belief in the justice of his cause. Happily he was not entirely without encouragement from the chiefs of his own profession, for just at the time when the outside world was decrying him most strenuously, the Academy elected him an Associate, an action that to modern critics of the retrograde policy of that institution must seem quite inexplicable. This election was, however, quashed, because he was discovered to be under the age at which admission was possible; and it was not till 1853 that he was again chosen. By this time he had added to the list of his paintings, his exquisite "Ophelia," "The Huguenot," "The Proscribed Royalist," and "The Order of Release," all works of the highest value, and regarded to-day as plain proofs of a quite extraordinary ability. They fared badly then at the hands of the critics, who did not take the trouble to understand their significance, and fastened instead upon trivial imperfections that had no importance whatever.

For about ten years he remained faithful to the Pre-Raphaelite creed, and made no serious attempt to modify his methods. During this period appeared his "Portrait of Mr Ruskin," "The Rescue," "Autumn Leaves," "The Blind Girl," "Sir Isumbras at the Ford," "The Vale of Rest," and "Apple Blossoms," of which the last two are to be reckoned as to some extent transitional, leading the way to the later changes in both his theory and practice. What was to be the nature of these changes was foreshadowed by "The Eve of St Agnes," shown at the Academy in 1863, the year before his advancement to

the rank of Royal Academician. After this he wavered
for a while between recollections of his earlier style, and a
very definite desire to find other ways of expressing himself, between the elaborate precision of "Leisure Hours,"
and "Swallow! Swallow!" the matter-of-fact of "Asleep"
and "Awake," the grim imagination of "The Enemy
sowing Tares," the elegant formality of "The Minuet," and
the technical freedom of "Joan of Arc" and "Esther."

The variations in his production at this time, implied a
degree of uncertainty in his idea as to the course which
it would be best for him to adopt, a hesitation about the
way in which he would most profitably occupy himself
after the abandonment of those details of his boyish faith
that had served their purpose, and had ceased to be
essential to his advance. He was conscious of the possibilities that his wonderful command over his materials
opened up to him, and he knew that his years of devoted
study had given him an equipment of knowledge that
would serve him in any emergency; what he was seeking
was the exact form in which to cast his efforts so as to
allow full scope to his abilities and to make indisputable
that wide popularity which was coming to him at last.

There was no hesitation about the avowal of his new
views when finally he did make up his mind. With a
suddenness that was absolutely startling, he abandoned
the close and careful realism that marked in such canvases
as "Asleep," "Awake," and "The Minuet," the still-
continuing influence of his Pre-Raphaelite conviction, and
chose instead the riotous freedom of touch, and the happy
readiness of suggestion that make his "Souvenir of Velasquez," "Rosalind and Celia," and "Stella," so impressive.
The dramatic point of this change is that a year sufficed
to bring it into active operation. In 1867 he was still
anxious to work out bit by bit and part by part every
fact that his subject might present, and, in his zeal for
naturalism, to leave no chance of mistake about the exact

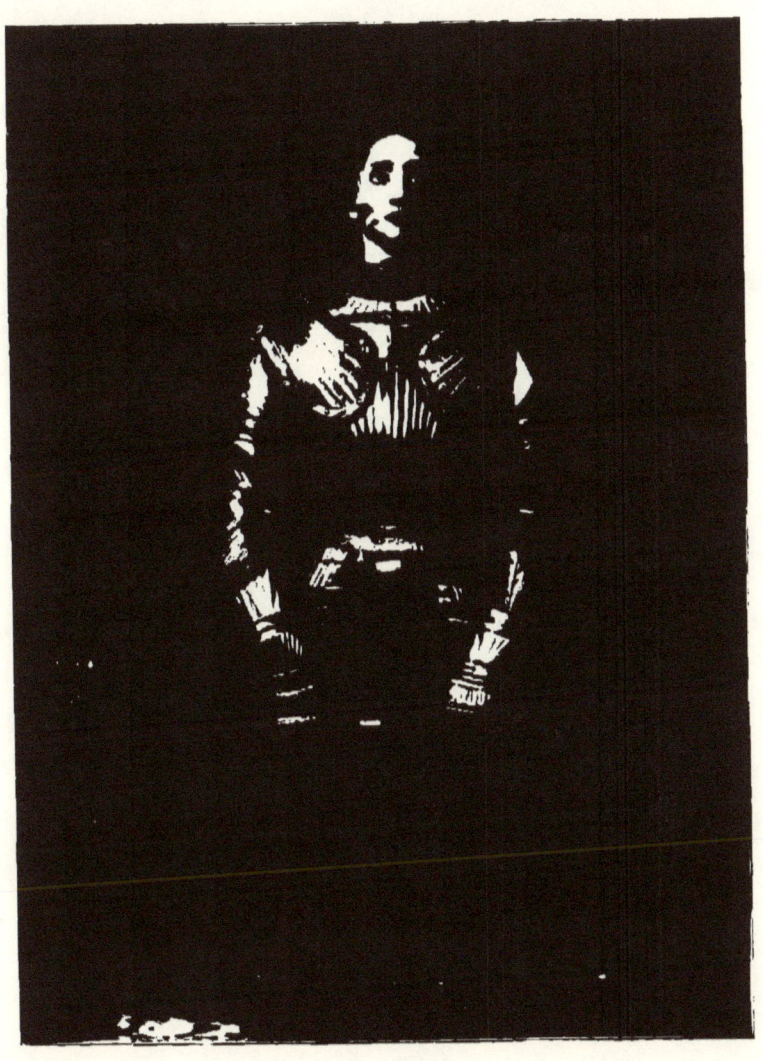

JOAN OF ARC

meaning of his treatment; in 1868 he had thrown himself heart and soul into the task of persuading his admirers to accept hints in the place of plain statements, and to understand subtle compromises with nature, instead of direct transcriptions of her assertions. He knew so well what she had to say, that he could trust himself to summarise, to avoid minute explanations in telling her story, and yet to miss nothing of its truth.

Thenceforward his progress was an almost unbroken series of successes, gained by superb mastery of craftsmanship, and by the splendid confidence in himself that put his intentions always beyond the possibility of doubt. With few exceptions his pictures, to the end of his life, were worthy to rank with the best that the British school can show, great in accomplishment, admirable in style, and attractive always by their frankness of manner and purity of motive. In some ways he enlarged his borders, for in 1871 he made, with "Chill October," his first digression into landscape without figures, and began that array of important studies of the open air, which are to be reckoned as the plainest evidences of his limitless patience and searching power of observation.

As a portrait painter, also, he developed superlative gifts, adding year by year to a collection of masterpieces unequalled by any of his contemporaries. He was fortunate in his sitters, and the list of his productions in this branch of art includes a large proportion of the most beautiful women and distingushed men who have graced the latter half of the century. He immortalised impartially leaders of fashion, pretty children, noted politicians, and people eminent in many professions; and in his rendering of these various types he missed nothing of the individuality and distinctive character with which each one was endowed. Here especially his Pre-Raphaelite training stood him in good stead; for the habit of close analysis and careful investigation had been so impressed upon him by the experiences of his youth that his instinctive judgment was now perfectly reliable, and his ability to decide promptly and with certainty about the aspects of his subject which were fittest for pictorial record had become absolutely complete.

In this succession of portraits some stand out commandingly as notable performances even for an artist, who was always distinguished—for example, "Mrs Bischoffsheim," "Miss Eveleen Tennant," "Mrs Jopling," "Mrs Perugini," "Sir Henry Irving," "The Right Hon. W. E. Gladstone (1885)," "J. C. Hook, R.A.," and "The Marquis of Salisbury," marking great moments in his career; just as from time to time figure compositions of rare importance, like "The North-West Passage," "Effie Deans," "The Princes in the Tower," and "Speak! Speak!" punctuated the progress of his intellectual and imaginative evolution. He was always, to the last day of his life, ambitious and eager to grapple with problems of technical expression. Courage to face the supreme difficulties of his profession never failed him. He had no idea of avoiding responsibilities, or of finding in an easy convention a way to evade his duty to art; and he tried consistently to bring his production up to the high level that would satisfy his ideals. When he missed his aim—and there is no such thing as unvarying success for any artist—it was not for want of thought or sincere effort, but rather from overanxiety. He once said of himself, "I may honestly say that I never consciously put an idle touch upon canvas, and that I have always been earnest and hard-working; yet the worst pictures I ever painted in my life are those into which I threw most trouble and labour"; and in these few words he summed up his whole history.

It was characteristic of him that the honours which were heaped upon him in his later years should have diminished neither the strength of his work nor the charm of his personality. Affectation or self-consciousness were the

J. C. HOOK, R.A.

last things that were possible to such a nature with its almost boyish energy and magnificent vitality. Yet he had every reason to be proud of success that had come to him, not by fortunate chance, but as a result of his own tenacity. He was made an Officer of the Legion of Honour, and received the Medaille d'Honneur at the Paris International Exhibition in 1878; the degree of D.C.L. was conferred upon him at Oxford in 1880, and at Durham in 1893; he was elected a Trustee of the National Portrait Gallery in 1881, a Foreign Associate of the Académie des Beaux Arts in 1882, and President of the Royal Academy in 1896; he was created a Baronet in 1885, and an Officer of the Order of Leopold in 1895; and was, besides, an Officer of the Order of St Maurice, and the Prussian Order "Pour la Mérite," and a member of the Academies of Vienna, Belgium, Antwerp, and of St Luke, Rome, and San Fernando, Madrid. He was one of the few Englishmen invited to contribute his portrait to the great collection of pictures of artists painted by themselves in the Uffizi Gallery at Florence. Such a record proves most cogently the manner in which the public estimate of his capacity changed as years went on; it is instructive to compare its unanimity of recognition with the story of the time when art teachers were urging their pupils to greet the name of Millais with hisses, and were holding up his work, and that of his associates, to the bitterest execration.

The post of President of the Royal Academy he held for only six months, for he succeeded Lord Leighton on February 20th, 1896, and died on 13th of August in the same year. His election, however, rounded off appropriately that long association with the Academy to which he referred in his speech at the 1895 banquet, at which he presided in the absence of Lord Leighton. "I must tell you briefly my connection with this Academy. I entered the Antique School as a probationer, when I was eleven

C

years of age; then became a student in the Life School; and I have risen from stage to stage until I reached the position I now hold of Royal Academician: so that, man and boy, I have been intimately connected with this Academy for more than half-a-century. I have received here a free education as an artist—an advantage any lad may enjoy who can pass a qualifying examination—and I owe the Academy a debt of gratitude I never can repay. I can, however, make this return—I can give it my love. I love everything belonging to it, the casts I have drawn from as a boy, the books I have consulted in our Library, the very benches I have sat on." No other teaching institution had, indeed, had any part in his education; no other art society had, by throwing over him the aegis of its influence, given him invaluable assistance at a moment when the world was against him; and in no other direction had such practical belief in the greatness of his future been manifested. Truly, he owed a debt of gratitude to the Academy, and he repaid it by being ever one of its most active supporters, and by doing infinite credit to its best traditions.

His death not only left a gap in the ranks of art, but it also took away, while he was yet in the full enjoyment of his powers, a man whose sterling qualities had attracted a host of friends. His frankness and honesty, his geniality and kindliness, and, above all, his manly wholesomeness, without taint of modern decadence or morbidity, endeared him to everyone with whom he came in contact. He was typically English, in the best sense, with all the physical and mental attributes that have enabled our race to dominate the world, a lover of the country, a good shot, a keen fisherman, and a fearless horseman. The very look of him, with his stalwart, well set-up figure, and handsome, self-reliant face, conveyed the impression of perfect health of mind and body, and declared the inexhaustible vigour of his nature.

A FORERUNNER

His life-long instinct was to fight strenuously against everything that looked like injustice or oppression, and in the Academy he championed assiduously every cause that seemed to him to lack its due measure of support. Especially was he an advocate of generous encouragement for the great school of black and white drawing that has sprung up of recent years; and it was his constant desire to see the illustrator accorded something of the official recognition which has hitherto been reserved, unfairly, as he argued, for painters and sculptors only—a desire that had its origin in that love of illustrative work which was so happily exemplified by his own ample achievement in black and white.

There was something peculiarly pathetic in the fact that his life should have ended just when he had reached the position that must have seemed to him, after his long and intimate connection with the Academy, the most honourable to which he could aspire. To be the head of the institution that he loved so well, and to be hailed as chief in the place that had seen every stage of his development, from childhood to ripe maturity, could not fail to be anything but exquisitely gratifying to a man of his nature. But almost at the moment of his election it appeared that there was little time left him in which to enjoy the honour that had crowned his many years of devotion to the great principles of art. The fatal disease that had gripped him a little while before was not to be shaken off, and was sapping rapidly and effectually even his superb vitality. He worked on, however, almost to the end, hopeful even in the midst of suffering, active in carrying out the duties of his office, and busy as ever with the canvases that crowded his studio. He was fully represented in the Academy Exhibition of 1896, by a group of portraits, and by a picture, " A Forerunner," which showed no sign of failing strength or of any relaxation in his grasp of the essentials of his craft.

Then, with painful suddenness, came the verdict of his doctors, that his case was hopeless. The throat trouble, that had been growing month by month more acute and distressing, was pronounced to be cancer and incurable. In June the disease had made such strides that the end seemed to be imminent, but an operation gave him some relief, and his life was prolonged till the middle of August, when at last death released him from his agony. He passed away at the house in Palace Gate, Kensington, that had been the scene of the many triumphs of his later years, dying as he had lived, full of courage and patience, fearing nothing, and meeting his fate with cheerful resignation. On August 20th, he was buried in St Paul's Cathedral, beside his old friend Lord Leighton, whom only a few months before he had helped to lay to rest.

SIR JOHN E. MILLAIS, BART.

CHAPTER III

T HE opportunities that have been afforded for the proper appreciation of the life-work of Sir John Millais have fortunately been both interesting and adequate. As it was particularly important that the value of his intervention in the aesthetic developments of the last fifty years should be thoroughly understood, and that there should be no doubt in the public mind about the significance of his contribution to modern art history, we may fairly congratulate ourselves on the fact that the whole sequence of effort should have been illustrated more than once by comprehensive and exhaustive exhibitions. In this way a later generation has been made familiar with those earlier stages of his practice, which must be considered before the meaning of his more recent performances can be fully realised; and to the present-day art-lover, the foundations of his aesthetic belief have been revealed in their right relation to the superstructure built upon them.

In the galleries of the Fine Art Society in 1881, at the Grosvenor Gallery in 1886, at the Manchester Art Treasures Exhibition in 1887, at the Academy in 1898, the story of the artist's life was told with all possible cogency by the aid of his own pictures, gathered together and placed in instructive juxtaposition. The canvases with which he challenged, in the fifties, the opposition of the older men, the later works which marked the victory of the Pre-Raphaelites, and the many masterpieces that brought him at last to his position of assured pre-eminence, provided in these shows exquisite proofs of his capacity, and summar-

37

ised for the benefit of people who had been unable to follow his progress step by step, the steady working out of his intentions. Necessarily, it was impossible in any exhibition to collect more than a moderate proportion of an output that totalled over three hundred and fifty in oil paintings alone, without taking into account any of that mass of black and white drawings with which he is also to be credited. But at the Grosvenor Gallery, and again at the Academy, enough of his work was shown to make clear his aesthetic purpose, and to leave no question about his right to attention.

Both collections had the merit of justifying quite completely the claim, which has so often been advanced on behalf of the artist, that his precocity was almost without parallel. They left no room for doubt concerning the reality of his command over technical intricacies at an age when most students have scarcely begun to think about applying to independent practice the knowledge acquired during their school training, and proved him to be possessed, even as a lad, of an insight into the details of his profession which comes as a rule only to the mature mind. The precocity that they revealed was not merely that of performance, an early acquirement of the devices of craftsmanship; it was, as well, a surprising completeness of conviction about the application of executive methods to the illustration of well-considered principles. There was nothing tentative or undecided about the pictures which began the record of his working life; they were essentially the efforts of a man who knew his own mind, and wished to impress upon other people ideas that he had formed in perfect good faith.

Really the only period during which he worked, as students will, without reasoning about the meaning of what he was doing, and content simply to reflect the view of others, was when he was between fourteen and eighteen. He had not freed himself then from the taint of the times.

The influence of the bastard "grand style" with which the men about him were afflicted was for a little while powerful enough to carry him into extravagances, and to delay the shaping of his individuality. His paintings before 1848 were quite in the fashion of the moment, designed to display his facility in composition and his skill in mechanism, with something of the violence of B. R. Haydon, the gorgeousness of Etty, the pedantry of Maclise, and with touches of the mannerism of many other artists who were then doing their best—or worst—for English Art. Etty certainly occupied his thoughts when he produced " Cymon and Iphigenia," which he seems to have begun when he was about seventeen, though he did not finish it until 1851 ; and there is a strong suggestion of Haydon in the strain and theatrical pose of " Pizarro seizing the Inca of Peru." More of his real self appeared in the enormous picture, " The Widow bestowing her Mite," prepared for the Westminster Hall Exhibition, and the six lunettes which he executed for the Judge's Lodgings at Leeds in 1847; more self-restraint and better judgment. They showed that he was beginning to think for himself, with less dependence upon the arbitrary rules laid down by the convention-mongers who were ready to welcome him as of their company. The lunettes, which now hang in the Corporation Art Gallery at Leeds, were, indeed, distinctly meritorious as attempts in serious design ; and " The Widow bestowing her Mite," though hardly equal in carrying out to its great intention, was very interesting as a display of youthful ambition. This picture, by the way, no longer exists in its complete form ; it was bought by a dealer who cut it in two: one piece is now at Tynemouth, the other in America.

In the following year he exhibited at the Academy a portrait of " W. Hugh Fenn," and at the British Institution, his gold medal picture. Meanwhile the new influence was coming into his life, and, under the stimulus of a fresh conviction, he was preparing for that radical change of direction which was to make his future work so important. Pre-Raphaelitism was to be henceforth his guiding principle, and the assertion of the highest truths of art was to be his aim. So he agreed with Rossetti and Holman Hunt that they should each choose a subject from "Isabella and the Pot of Basil," the poem by Keats, and paint it with absolute fidelity to the tenets of their common creed, with strict regard for facts, and without departing in the smallest degree from nature. Out of this agreement came the picture which was the only contribution by Millais to the Academy of 1849.

It was characteristic of him that he should be the only one of the three to fulfil his part of the arrangement. While the others were troubling with laborious preparations, he had made up his mind about the treatment of the motive he had chosen, had settled every detail, and finally had carried to triumphant completion a very remarkable composition. This picture, his "Lorenzo and Isabella," with its amazing care in the rendering of textures and surfaces, its minute finish, its delicate colour, and its brilliancy of illumination, is uncompromising in its realism, and extraordinarily patient in its representation of the material selected. The various figures were painted from friends and relations of the young artist—from his sister-in-law, Mrs Hodgkinson, his father, the two Rossettis, Mrs F. G. Stephens, and some fellow-students. The reception accorded to the picture by the critics was on the whole not unfavourable, though it was pronounced to have "too much mannerism," and to be the work of a man "evidently enslaved by preference for a false style."

That Millais had made up his mind about the merits of such mannerism, and had a very pronounced belief in his "false style," was seen plainly enough a twelvemonth later when "Ferdinand lured by Ariel," the "Portrait of a Gentleman and his Grandchild," and "Christ in the House

THE PROSCRIBED ROYALIST

THE BLACK BRUNSWICKER

of his Parents," appeared at the Academy. The first of these three canvases illustrates the line from "The Tempest," "Where should this music be? i' the air, or the earth?" and represents Ferdinand walking in an open space before a wood, with Ariel and a crew of gauze-winged sprites hovering around him, a wonderful study of brilliant sunlight and luxuriant landscape detail, and as noteworthy for its quaintness of imagination as for its beauty of finish. It is, however, less ambitious than "Christ in the House of his Parents," in which all the resources of Pre-Raphaelitism were turned to good account, and the logic of the new creed was asserted with unquestion-ing faith. A verse in Zechariah, "And one shall say unto him, 'What are these wounds in thine hands?' Then he shall answer, 'Those with which I was wounded in the house of my friends,'" provided the motive; and the same exact observation that gave significance to "Lorenzo and Isabella" controlled the execution.

As a religious painting of a Holy Family this work was, from the point of view of the period, to be assigned to "the lowest depths of what is mean, odious, repulsive, and repelling." It certainly shows no respect for any of the traditions which were then popularly supposed to call for the unquestioning support of every artist, for the spirit by which was inspired such a composition, for instance, as Sir Charles Eastlake's "Christ lamenting over Jerusalem," a picture, now in the Tate Gallery, which explains very well the sort of feebleness that was in fashion in the middle of the century. Millais did not hesitate to put on one side all the namby-pamby prettiness and elegant affectation which governed the production of his contemporaries, and struck out for himself in a very different direction. He laid the scene of his story in the house of Joseph, and, to quote another critic, associated the characters of the sacred story "with the meanest details of a carpenter's shop, with no conceivable omission of misery, of dirt, and even of

disease, all finished with the same loathsome minuteness."
The child Christ stands before the carpenter's bench with
the Virgin kneeling beside him preparing to bind up
with a piece of linen a wound in his hand, at which Joseph,
leaning forward from the end of the bench, is looking. St
Anne in the background is picking up a pair of pincers,
and beside Joseph is John the Baptist coming towards the
central group with a bowl of water in his hands. An
assistant on the other side of the picture watches the
incident gravely.

The keynote of the whole composition is its earnest
symbolism. Every one of the lovingly-laboured details
explains something of the story, the tools on the wall, the
dove perched on the ladder, and the sheep, typifying the
faithful, and the wattled fence, an emblem of the Church,
which are seen through the doorway; while in the meadow
beyond is placed a well as a symbol of Truth. In its
imaginative qualities, the picture is not less masterly than
in its technical accuracy, and excites as much wonder by
the depth of thought it reveals as by its astonishing accomplishment. It is the greatest of all the artist's earlier
works, marking definitely his emancipation from the
influences of his student days, and his development in
craftsmanship.

He exhibited next "The Woodman's Daughter," which
he had begun in 1849, and with it "Mariana in the Moated
Grange," and "The Return of the Dove to the Ark," three
pictures of medium size, which excited the intense in-
dignation of the commentators on the art work of the
year, and drew from Mr Ruskin the first eloquent expression of his approval of the purpose of the Brotherhood,
and his advocacy of the claim of Millais and his friends
to the support of everyone who had honest convictions
about artistic questions. To the same date belongs "The
Bridesmaid," known at one time as "All Hallow's E'en,"
an exquisite study of a girl passing, in accordance with

THE BRIDESMAID

the old superstition, a piece of bride-cake through a ring. This canvas is now in the Fitzwilliam Museum at Cambridge, to which it was presented in 1888 by Mr T. R. Harding.

In 1852 he gave an astonishing display of his ability ; for he had at the Academy " Ophelia," and " The Huguenot "— which was then called " A Huguenot, on St Bartholomew's Day, refusing to shield himself from Danger by wearing the Roman Catholic Badge,"—as well as a portrait of Mrs Coventry Patmore, and another portrait entitled " Memory." The " Ophelia," which is happily now the property of the nation, and hangs in the Tate Gallery, is an admirable example of his searching study of natural details, close and elaborate in its realisation of every part of the subject, and curiously true in its rendering of the subtle tones of brilliant daylight. The face of Ophelia was painted from Miss Siddal, who afterwards became the wife of Dante Gabriel Rossetti, and the landscape setting was exactly copied from a bit of the Ewell River, near Kingston. With the " Huguenot," though he did not succeed in silencing the whole of his detractors, he gained the heart of the public. The pathos of the subject, and the dramatic strength of its story, were well calculated to persuade everyone who could judge without bias, and could feel the charm of the painting even through its unaccustomed style. While the picture was on exhibition it was always surrounded by a crowd, and it was sold, for £150, to a dealer, who afterwards gave the artist an extra £50 because it brought considerable profit when engraved.

During the next three years his chief productions were " The Proscribed Royalist," " The Order of Release," " The Portrait of Mr Ruskin," and " The Rescue." Of these the most fortunate, both in idea and execution, is " The Order of Release," a Highland woman bringing in triumph to the prison in which her husband is confined, the signed authority for his restoration to freedom. The little drama is most convincingly played, and the different characters, even to the collie dog that leaps up to lick his master's hand, perform their parts with complete sincerity. There is hardly so much conviction in "The Proscribed Royalist," a Puritan maiden visiting her Cavalier lover who is hiding in a hollow oak tree: there is even an obvious touch of artificiality; but as a display of superb industry, and exquisite management of the intricacies of woodland scenery, this picture is certainly to be ranked among the artist's best.

The same exquisite industry made his "Portrait of Mr Ruskin" supremely valuable as a technical achievement. He reached in it the highest level of pure Pre-Raphaelitism, and showed most surely the perfection of the strict principles by which his artistic personality had been shaped. The great critic stands bare-headed and almost in profile on the rocky bank beside the waterfall of Glenfinlas, in the Highlands, posing easily and naturally; and the artist has painted both the figure and its surroundings with searching knowledge. The landscape background especially, "pure, vivid, and solid as a sincere and spontaneous mode of painting could make it," to quote a contemporary criticism from the *Athenæum*, can only be described as magnificent, finer even than the leafy setting of the "Ophelia." This portrait was not seen in public until 1881, when it was included in the collection at the galleries of the Fine Art Society. Two other small pictures, "Waiting," and "A Highland Lassie," both unexhibited, are to be assigned to the year 1854. The "Highland Lassie" was a study for "Waiting," which is also known as "A Girl at a Stile." It was painted from the lady, Miss Euphemia Chalmers Gray, whom he married in 1855.

Concerning the merits of "The Rescue," most people seem to have agreed. Mr Ruskin pronounced it to be

A HIGHLAND LASSIE

THE KNIGHT ERRANT

the only great picture of its year, and praised it as much on account of its truth as of its sentiment; while another critic described it as "one of those subjects which illustrate our ideal of the proper functions of art." The incident, a fireman rescuing three young children from a burning house, on the staircase of which kneels their mother, waiting to take them from his arms, was exactly calculated to appeal to the popular fancy; and the manner in which the artist studied and realised the effects of tone and colour made the work, as an essay in technicalities, quite unusually important. It was painted in great haste, and was finished only just in time for exhibition in the 1855 Academy; but the speed with which it was executed gave it a degree of vigour thoroughly appropriate to a subject so filled with action.

As he had shown nothing in 1854, and only this one canvas in 1855, Millais took care to do himself more ample justice in the following year. "Autumn Leaves" appeared then, and with it "The Random Shot," "Peace Concluded, 1856," "The Blind Girl," and the "Portrait of a Gentleman," also known as "The Picture Book." The especial subtlety of "Autumn Leaves," which is now rightly admired as one of the most perfect pieces of poetic and tender sentiment that he ever produced, was not immediately appreciated, and the symbolism of the composition was not readily understood; but the expert observers saw in it qualities of the noblest kind, and a judgment of atmospheric effects such as no other living man could be said to possess. Mr Ruskin ranked "Autumn Leaves" and "Peace Concluded" among the masterpieces of the world, and with generous enthusiasm asserted that "Titian himself could hardly head him now." "The Random Shot," or, as it was first called, "L'Enfant du Régiment," represents an incident in the French Revolution: a child, accidentally wounded, lying upon a monument in a church that is being defended by some soldiers who are seen firing from

a window. The monument was painted from the tomb of
Sir Gervaise Allard, in the old church at Winchelsea, where
the artist was staying in the autumn of 1855. "The Blind
Girl," another of his minute realisations of landscape
details, and notable as well for its true and natural pathos
was produced at the same time. The village of Winchelsea
is seen on the hill behind the figures. "Pot-Pourri," a
small picture of two young girls also belongs to this year.

At the next Academy exhibition his chief work was "Sir
Isumbras at the Ford," originally known as "A Dream of
the Past," an allegory susceptible of many interpretations,
and one that the public had some difficulty in understanding. It was freely attacked and discussed, and it
drew down a measure of denunciation from Mr Ruskin,
who summed it up as "a rough sketch of a great subject,"
and described it as "not merely a Fall—it is Catastrophe."
Yet its fineness of design, and beauty of twilight effect
have placed it, according to the modern estimate of the
artist's achievement, among the best of his canvases. It
takes certainly a much higher position than "The Escape
of a Heretic," a piece of plain melodrama, or "News from
Home," a Highlander reading a letter as he sits on the
trenches at the Crimea, both of which were with it at the
Academy. Two heads, which were in the 1898 exhibition
at Burlington House, were painted at this time, and have
a special interest because they are the only pictures by
Millais which suggest that he was ever perceptibly influenced by Rossetti.

There was another break in the sequence of his contributions to the Academy, in 1858; and it was not till
the following spring that "The Vale of Rest" shocked
the public, that, after having become accustomed to Millais
the Pre-Raphaelite, now found themselves called upon to
accept him in quite another guise, as a symbolist and
imaginative moralist. He had entered upon his transition,
and had moved far from the literalism of "Christ in the

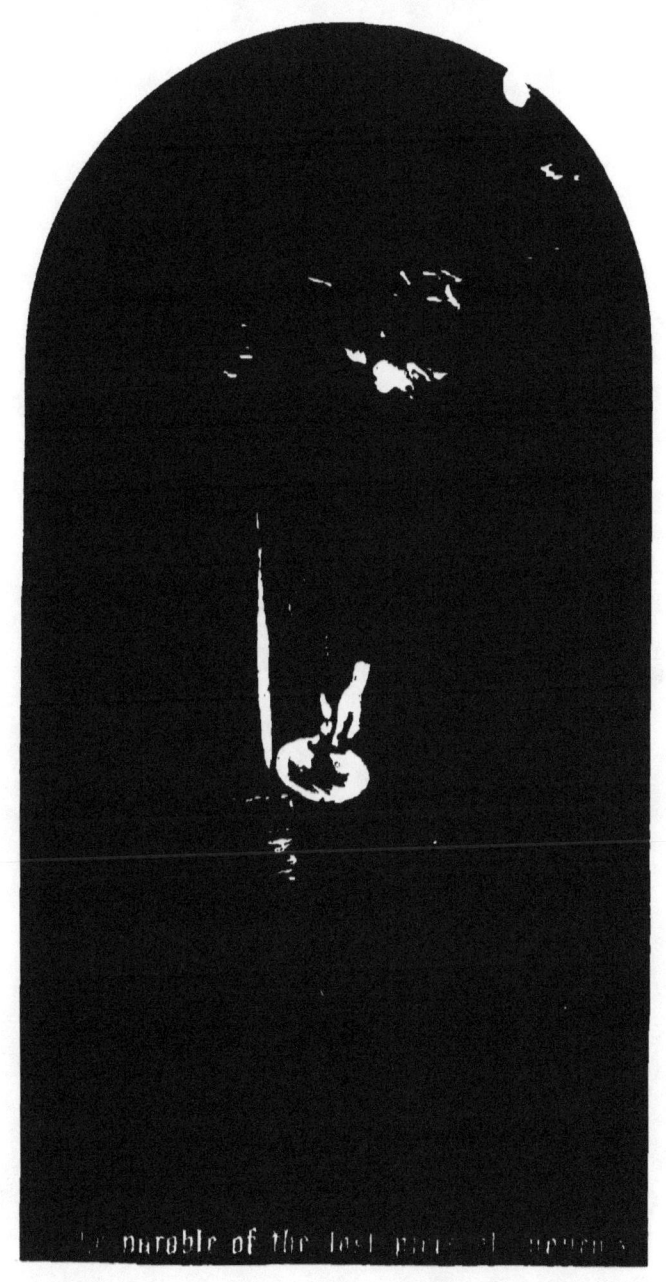

The parable of the lost piece of money

House of his Parents," and the obvious actuality of "Ophelia," towards that coming declaration of those individual preferences which were to guide him in the work of the latter half of his life. "The Vale of Rest" is said to have been of all his paintings the one most highly estimated by the artist; and it is justly reckoned with "Lorenzo and Isabella," "Autumn Leaves," "Chill October," "The North-West Passage," and the "Yeoman of the Guard," as among the chief successes of his career. It certainly overshadows the canvases that accompanied it to the Academy, "The Love of James I. of Scotland," and "Apple Blossoms," which was then called "Spring Flowers." This last work was rather aptly attacked by Mr Ruskin as "a fierce and rigid orchard," but he admitted its indisputable excellence of handling and its real power. It is somewhat uncompromising in aspect, and is more to be commended as an exercise in realism than because it possesses those great pictorial virtues that distinguish "The Vale of Rest."

Between 1859 and 1863 the artist produced more than a dozen things, most of which were of minor interest. Among them was "The Black Brunswicker," a picture of the same class as "The Huguenot," and "The Proscribed Royalist," but scarcely so successful either in feeling or performance. It was, however, popular enough at the time, and had a great vogue as an engraving. The face of the girl, who tries to delay the parting between herself and her hussar lover, was painted from the daughter of Charles Dickens, now Mrs Perugini. A larger canvas, "The Ransom," was at the Academy in 1862, with "Trust Me," and another work, "The Parable of the Lost Piece of Money," which was destroyed not long afterwards by an explosion in the house of Baron Marrochetti, where it was hanging. "The White Cockade," a small painting which repeated one of his earlier black and white drawings, was shown in the same year at the

French Gallery; and he finished several other small wc
of which "The Bride" may be taken as an example.

The Academy in 1863 is memorable because it inclu
not only his "Eve of St Agnes," with its splendid ren
ing of rich textures and deep tones of cool colour,
also "My First Sermon," a child sitting in a pew at chu
and fascinated by the eloquence of a preacher on wl
though he is not seen in the picture, her gaze is fi
This picture, which achieved immediately an enorn
amount of popularity, was practically the first of
long series of studies of child-life with which Mi
put himself into successful competition with Sir Jo:
Reynolds, and gained a place in the affections of
public that is only reserved for men who know exa
what will appeal to the tenderest human emot:
Another picture of children, "The Wolf's Den," wa
the same exhibition; but this one was less simple,
was more notable for brilliancy of technique than
charm of subject.

By the success of "My First Sermon" he was indi
to paint for the next year's exhibition a companion su
"My Second Sermon," the same child, in the same
and wearing the red cloak that appeared in the c
picture, but this time unimpressed by the novelty of
surroundings. She has found the discourse a little be
her understanding, and has gone to sleep in all innoce
A larger picture, of two children, in red velvet dre
sitting on a carpeted floor with an elaborately patte
leather screen behind them, and a bowl of gold fis
their feet, was shown at the same time under the
"Leisure Hours"; and a couple of portraits also appe
But besides these Academy contributions he produce
1864 "The Conjuror," "Charlie is My Darling," and anc
portrait, of a son of Tom Taylor.

During the next twelve months he was not
industrious, for he exhibited at the Academy "

MY FIRST SERMON

MY SECOND SERMON

THE MINUET

nemy Sowing Tares," "Joan of Arc," "Esther," "The
omans leaving Britain," and "Swallow! Swallow!"
nd two other canvases at the French Gallery. Neither
The Romans leaving Britain," nor "Swallow! Swallow!"
an be accounted as anything but indifferent illustrations
f his capacity: the one is weak and inconclusive; the
ther violent in colour and wanting in charm; and "Joan
f Arc," strong though it is as a piece of pure painting,
 really nothing but a clever costume study. But "The
nemy Sowing Tares" has a dramatic significance that
 rare even in his most imaginative efforts, an amount of
itellectual purpose greater than almost any of his other
ictures can be credited with. He had treated the same
ubject as one of the illustrations to a book, "The Parables
f Our Lord," which was published about 1864. The figure
f the sower personifies the Evil One, who is scattering the
eed with an expression of grim pleasure in ill-doing, while
round him slink and crawl prowling things dimly seen
1 the gloom of night. The artist, who had just been
iromoted to the rank of Royal Academician, intended
his to be his Diploma picture; but when he offered it to
he Council it was, strangely, enough, not appreciated,
nd therefore refused. A little later on he deposited the
Souvenir of Velasquez" instead.

As a brilliant contrast to the strange fancy of "The
nemy Sowing Tares," there appeared in 1867 one of
he brightest and most delightful of his paintings, "The
Minuet." A young child in a scarlet dress, which she
iolds up with a due sense of importance, is just beginning
 dance in a room sumptuously hung with tapestries that
nake an effective background to her gay attire. Her
[uaint air of responsibility, and her childish stateliness, are
)articularly attractive, and are suggested by the artist with
:harming freshness and yet with just the right hint of old-
ashioned formality. With this delicate expression of
/outhful graces was exhibited his "Jephthah," a great and

D

serious composition, representing the champion of Israel,
seated in his house with his daughter beside him; and,
as well, two small pictures, "Asleep," and "Awake," that,
in the minute and elaborate treatment of accessories, and
in the precision of touch employed to define and realise
every detail, reverted almost to the unsparing labour of
his Pre-Raphaelite days.

But they really marked finally and distinctly the end
of his early methods, and might almost have been painted
with the deliberate intention of emphasising the change
in his technical manner that was immediately at hand.
With them he bade farewell to the executive devices
that had served him so well in the past, and rounded off
that busy period of his life in which were included
the brilliant successes of his youth, the struggles of his
early manhood, and the steady progress from misunder-
standing and misrepresentation to the general and sincere
acceptance which it was his fortune to gain before he had
reached middle age.

ASLEEP

JUST AWAKE.

CHAPTER IV

WHEN, in the Academy exhibition of 1868, people, who had retained vivid recollections of the pictures with which their favourite, Millais, had delighted them only a year before, looked to see what were the canvases he had prepared to carry on the impression created by " Asleep," " Awake," and " The Minuet," something of a shock must have been experienced by them. They had known him last as a careful and exact manipulator, a lover of high finish, and an exponent of all the little subtleties of nature ; ´ when they met him again after the brief interval of a twelvemonth they found him a robust impressionist, glorying in his power to give by a few large and decisive touches a significant summary of many facts, and eager to render great effects rather than minutely analysed and carefully selected details. From "The Minuet" to the "Souvenir of Velasquez" was a change that could not be mistaken or explained away. It meant that he had abandoned the restrictions of the Pre-Raphaelite method and had begun to apply its principles in such a way that he could aim at the highest flights of executive expression.

This change was illustrated not only by the " Souvenir of Velasquez," but as well by the other pictures that he sent to the Academy with this delightful instance of his understanding of childish character. There was the same technical spirit in " Rosalind and Celia," in " Stella," a splendidly vigorous painting of a half-length figure, in " Pilgrims to St Paul's," now better known as " Greenwich Pensioners at the Tomb of Nelson," and in " The Sisters,".

a portrait group of his three daughters in white and blue dresses set against a background of pink and white azaleas.' To the same year belong also some smaller works, among them another with the title, "The Bride," which was used two or three times by the artist at different periods.

That his new manner was not the result of a momentary fancy, or of a passing desire for experiment, was seen clearly next year when his portrait of "Nina, daughter of F. Lehmann, Esq." was exhibited; for in this canvas he showed an amount of mastery that surpassed even the certainty and ready contrivance of the "Souvenir of Velasquez"; and another piece of masculine brush-work, "Vanessa," a companion to the "Stella" that had been seen in the previous exhibition, proved that the wish to rival the great executants of other schools had possessed him completely. "The Gambler's Wife," a "Portrait of Sir John Fowler," and a couple of water-colours, completed the list of his contributions to the 1869 Academy. These were followed by a group that was as interesting for varied accomplishment as for the evidence it afforded of his unhesitating progress. It included "A Widow's Mite," which was a picture very different in its inspiration from his Westminster Hall design, "The Knight Errant," "A Flood," "The Boyhood of Raleigh," and two portraits.

Of these the most conspicuous were "The Boyhood of Raleigh," and "The Knight Errant." The first is to be regarded as one of his happiest pieces of sentiment, a pleasant romance related with natural charm, and with a touch of human feeling that makes it most persuasive. The figures of the young Raleigh and his companion, who are sitting on the old pier of a Devonshire seaport, listening to the tales of adventure told them by a sunburn sailor, are happily conceived, and the atmosphere of the whole picture is exactly appropriate. There is no straining after effect, no exaggeration, and the whole scheme is carried out with perfect consistency. In "The Knigh

THE MARTYR OF THE SOLWAY

THE BRIDE

Errant," romance of a more fanciful kind is attempted, a
story with a flavour of mediævalism that fits it well.
The picture, however, is remarkable especially because it
provides one of the few instances in which Millais set himself to paint the nude figure; and it has a technical interest
of an unusual sort because it puts beyond question his
ability to excel in a branch of practice that is universally
admitted to be exceptionally difficult, and to require the
rarest combination of knowledge and skill.   As a study
of flesh texture the figure of the maiden, who has been
stripped by robbers and bound to a tree, is worthy of all
praise; and as a piece of subtle yet glowing colour it is
comparable with the best efforts of the Venetian Masters.
The armour, too, of the Knight who is setting her free is
superbly handled.   Some of the quality of the work is,
perhaps, to be attributed to the comparative haste with
which it was painted; it is said to have been completed in
not more than six weeks.

A story is told with reference to this painting that is
worth quoting, especially as it helps to fix the date of
another of his productions.   In his first arrangement of
the figures he had turned the girl's head towards the
spectator, and had thereby injured appreciably the sentiment of the composition.   So dissatisfied was he with
the result that he was at first inclined to destroy the
picture; but, upon consideration, another way of solving
the difficulty was found.   The head was cut out and a
fresh piece of canvas sewn in.   On this he painted the
face as it now appears, in profile; and by the change he
greatly improved the pictorial effect.   The piece with the
original head was preserved, and is supposed, after having
been inserted in a larger canvas, to have been completed
as " The Martyr of the Solway."   This supposition is
certainly borne out by the strong similarity between the
pose of the martyr and that of the nude figure in " The
Knight Errant."

In 1871 he broke new ground, and, with "Cl
began that series of great landscapes to wh
while he devoted himself with unwavering ap
intense respect for nature. Until 1880 there
any break in the succession of these canvases,
to the Sea" and "Flowing to the River" appe
"Scotch Firs" and "Winter Fuel" in 1874, '
of the Moor" and "The Deserted Garden" in
the Hills and Far Away" in 1876, "The Soᵤ
Waters" in 1877, "St Martin's Summer" :
"Urquhart Castle" in 1879; but then there w
until 1888, when "Murthly Moss" was at tl
and "Christmas Eve" at Mr Maclean's galler;

These landscapes, however, represent a ve:
portion of the memorable pictures that mac
between the beginning of the seventies and '
the eighties specially distinguished even in hi
career. During these fifteen years he prod
hundred and fifty works of different kinds
them were many that mark the highest and
development of his art. With "Chill Octobᵤ
the Academy "Yes, or No?" "Victory, O Lorᵤ
nambulist," and the "Portrait of George Gr
1872 came his famous portrait group, "Hearts
which was hailed at the time with enthusi:
remained ever since in high favour with all
work. It is generally supposed to have beᵤ
rivalry of the famous picture of the Ladies
by Sir Joshua Reynolds, but it bears really
ficial resemblance to that celebrated canvas,
distinction far more to the inventiveness and
modern master than to any imitation of hi:
Some other portraits were exhibited with i:

Another splendid technical achievement, th
Mrs Bischoffsheim," belongs to the followin;
this he stamped himself as the indisputable

MRS BISCHOFFSHEIM

school, supreme in accomplishment, and alone in his marvellous command over the intricacies of executive practice.
Never before had he shown himself so consummately able,
or so confident in his extraordinary readiness of resource ;
and only occasionally in the years that followed can he
be said to have reached the same degree of perfection.
His admirable portraits of " Mrs Heugh " and " Sir William
Sterndale Bennett," and three pictures, " Early Days," " Oh,
that a Dream so long Enjoyed," and " New-Laid Eggs," a
pretty fancy painted from one of his daughters, were
hung in the same exhibition ; but their merits were to
some extent overshadowed by the superlative power of
" Mrs Bischoffsheim."

That this performance was not a happy accident, one
of those chance successes which sometimes come to an
artist as a result of a fortunate combination of circumstances, was put beyond doubt by the character of his
contributions to the 1874 Academy exhibition. He fully
maintained the high level of craftsmanship at which he had
arrived in the previous year, but he displayed his strength
in a large and ambitious composition, an important subject-
picture instead of a portrait. " The North-West Passage "
may fairly be reckoned as the most complete assertion of
his mature conviction that he ever put before the public.
Its motive was one calculated to appeal vividly to his
militant instincts, and was suited in every way to his
robust and energetic personality. The idea of indomitable
perseverance in the face of difficulties seemingly insurmountable, of tenacious effort to triumphantly accomplish
a great intention, was quite in accordance with his natural
sympathies; and the picture has therefore an inner
significance to which almost as much interest attaches as
to its outward aspect of unhesitating certainty. It is,
perhaps, a little unequal in execution, but parts of it are
magnificent, and especially the head of the old seaman,
who sits at the table and listens to the story of Arctic

exploration that is being read to him by the girl seated at his feet. The sitter for this splendid study of rugged age was Mr Trelawny, the friend of Shelley and Byron.

To the same year as "The North-West Passage" belong "The Picture of Health," a three-quarter-length figure of a young girl, with her hands in a muff, and long hair falling over her shoulders, standing in a garden; "A Day Dream"; a portrait of "The Hon. Walter Rothschild"; and "Still for a Moment," a vivacious picture of a child in a white pinafore, seated on the trunk of a fallen tree, with a little dog in her lap. These were followed by some more portraits, and by a couple of pictures, "No," and "The Crown of Love," which Mr Ruskin, in his notes on the Academy, dismissed as "sketches," though he admitted that "The Crown of Love" was, in dramatic sentiment, the chief canvas shown that season. But neither in 1875, nor in 1876, when "Forbidden Fruit" and "Getting Better" were exhibited, did Millais paint anything finer than his portrait of "Miss Eveleen Tennant," an amazing display of brilliant colour and strong tones, handled with great fluency and with a kind of riotous enjoyment of the chances that were afforded him by the characteristic picturesqueness of his subject.

His masterpiece for 1877 was the "Yeoman of the Guard," an even more riotous and gorgeous essay in strong colour than his chief work of the year before. The scarlet uniform with its lavish embroidery of black and gold, and its picturesque fashion, was something that exactly suited his fancy; and he revelled in his struggle with the many difficulties that such a technical problem presented to him. But there is little sign in the picture that he found this subject more than usually exacting. It is particularly noteworthy for its consistent and thorough treatment, for the sound judgment with which every detail both of the colour and the design has been managed; and it is not less interesting on account of the sensitive and characteristic

A YEOMAN OF THE GUARD

rendering of the worn old face of the model than as a piece of still life painting of quite extraordinary force. The year in which it was exhibited was one in which he was unusually prolific ; for with it he showed, at the Academy, his portrait of " The Earl of Shaftesbury " and a picture "Yes"; at the Grosvenor Gallery, "Stitch! Stitch!" and portraits of "The Marchioness of Ormonde," "Countess Grosvenor," and "Lady Beatrice Grosvenor"; at the King Street Gallery, his delightfully imagined " Effie Deans"; " Puss in Boots," at Mr Maclean's gallery ; and he painted, besides, his portrait of Carlyle, and a three-quarter-length picture of a girl to which he gave the title " Bright Eyes." These were not exhibited at the time.

At the Grosvenor Gallery appeared, in 1878, " A Good Resolve," a girl in a blue bodice and brown skirt, standing with her hand on an open Bible, and "Twins," a portrait group of the daughters of Mr T. R. Hoare; and at the Academy " The Princes in the Tower," a composition that has had a great success as an engraving; " A Jersey Lily," and a portrait. His " Bride of Lammermoor" was shown separately, at the King Street Gallery. Of the works completed in the following year, the best remembered is " Cherry Ripe," the most widely popular of all his pictures of children, and in some respects the daintiest and most fascinating illustration that he ever gave of a class of art production that requires particular delicacy and subtlety of expression. To the Academy he sent portraits of "Mr Gladstone," " Mrs S. H. Beddington," and " Mrs Arthur Kennard," and another of " Mrs Stibbard " to the Grosvenor Gallery.

There, too, was hung next spring his painting of " Mrs Jopling," an exquisite example of his most perfect and accomplished art, quiet, reserved, and simple, but not want-ing in meaning, and curiously exact in its suggestion of the charm that attaches to a gifted personality. The treatment of the sensitive face, refined and feminine, and yet full of decision, is so sure and judicious, so free from careless idealisation or thoughtless mannerism, that it can scarcely be too highly praised. The picture, altogether, is exceptional in its manner, combining with rare skill the noblest qualities of the artist's method with the best expression of his capacity for close observation. It was one of several fine things of the same class that he exhibited that year, contemporaneous with the likeness of himself painted for the Uffizi Gallery, and with the portraits of " The Right Hon. John Bright," " Miss Catherine Muriel Cowell Stepney," " Luther Holden, P.R.C.S.," and " Miss Hermione Schenley." All these, with a picture, called " Cuckoo," two children sitting in a wood, were at the Academy.

Indeed, during the first half of the eighties, portraits made up the bulk of his contributions to the exhibitions at Burlington House and the Grosvenor Gallery, while most of his subject-pictures were shown at one or other of the dealers' galleries. To the Academy he sent, in 1881, " The Rev. John Caird, D.D.," " Bishop Fraser," " Sir J. D. Astley," " Sir Gilbert Greenall," " Lord Wimborne," " The Earl of Beaconsfield," and only one subject-picture, his pretty " Cinderella "; and to the Grosvenor Gallery his exquisitely-handled portrait of " Mrs Perugini," whose face appears in several of his earlier works, and another subject-picture, " Sweetest Eyes were ever seen." In 1882 the Academy had his " Cardinal Newman," " Sir Henry Thompson," " Mrs James Stern," " Dorothy Thorpe," " Mrs Richard Budgett," " D. Thwaites," and " H.R.H. The Princess Marie of Edinburgh "; in 1883 his splendid study of " J. C. Hook, R.A.," " The Marquis of Salisbury," " T. H. Ismay," and " Charles Waring," two fancy portraits, " Love Birds," and "-Forget-me-not," and a subject, " The Grey Lady "; in 1884, " Sir Henry Irving," " Fleetwood Wilson," " Miss Scott," and a large picture, " An Idyll, 1745 "; and, in 1885, " Lady Peggy Primrose," " Simon Fraser," " Orphans," and the important canvas, " The

THOMAS CARLYLE

By permission of the Fine Art
Society, owners of the copyright

PRINCESS ELIZABETH IN PRISON
AT ST JAMES'S

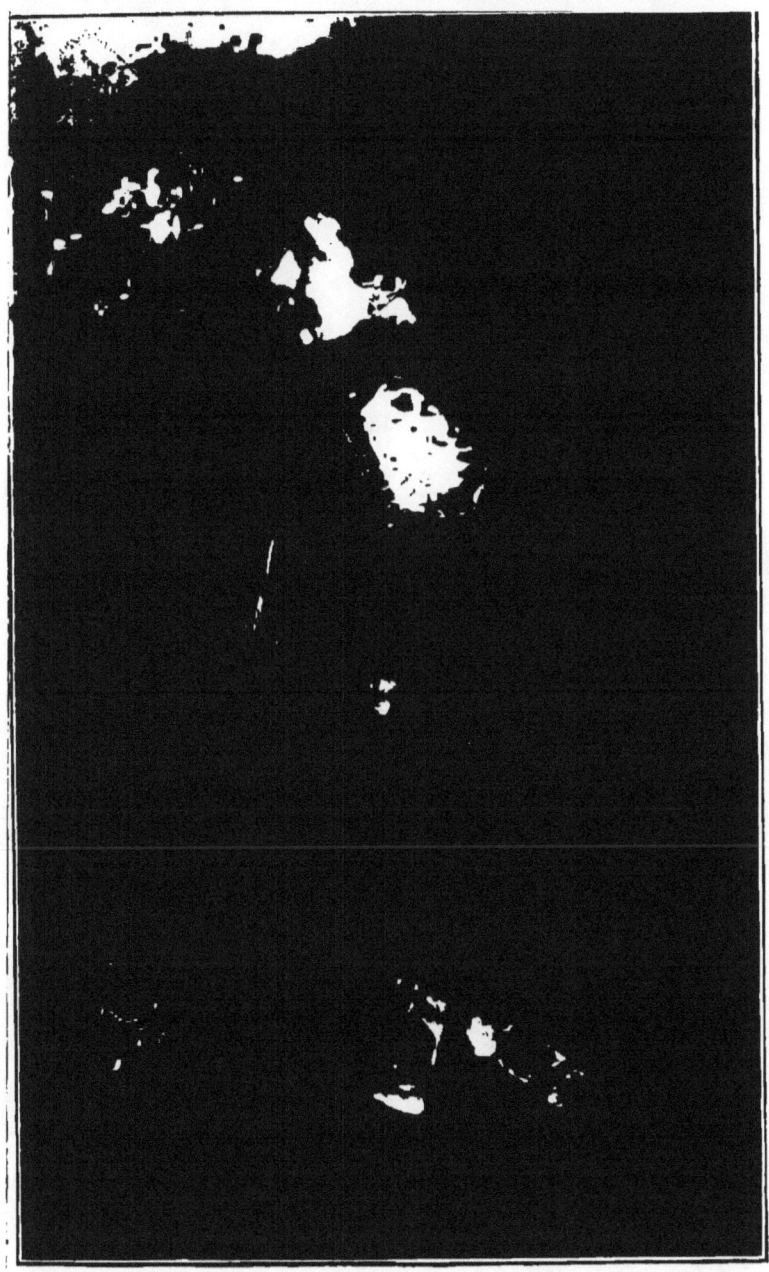

MRS PERUGINI

Ruling Passion," about which Mr Ruskin wrote at the time that he had never seen a modern work that filled him with more delight and admiration.

Meanwhile he had exhibited at the Grosvenor Gallery, "The Children of Octavius Moulton Barrett, Esq." and "Mrs Garrow-Whitby," in 1882; "For the Squire" in 1883; "Lady Campbell," whom he had painted before as Miss Nina Lehmann, and "The Marquess of Lorne," in 1884; and, in 1885, "Miss Margaret Millais" and "The Right Hon. W. E. Gladstone." The chief subject-pictures that during this period went to dealers' galleries were "The Princess Elizabeth," "Caller Herrin'," "The Captive," and "Dropped from the Nest," shown by the Fine Art Society; "Pomona," and "Olivia," by Messrs Tooth; "Little Miss Muffett," "Perfect Bliss," "A Message from the Sea," and "The Mistletoe Gatherer," by Mr Maclean; and "The Waif," by Messrs Dowdeswell. The Fine Art Society also exhibited, in 1881, his portrait of "Alfred, Lord Tennyson."

In 1886 a portrait of "T. O. Barlow, R.A." was at the Academy, but his other pictures went elsewhere, "Bubbles" to Messrs Tooth, and "Ruddier than the Cherry" and "Portia" to Mr Maclean. The following year was a fairly busy one, and examples of his work were seen in many directions. The Academy had three pictures, "Mercy; St Bartholomew's Day," "Lilacs," and "The Nest," besides portraits of "The Earl of Rosebery" and "The Marquis of Hartington"; the Grosvenor, portraits of "Lord Esher" and "Mrs Charles Stuart Wortley"; and Mr Maclean, "Allegro," "Penseroso," and "Clarissa." The largest of these, the "St Bartholomew's Day," is not to be reckoned as one of his best pictures; it is a little too obviously a costume study.

For the next five years his more important canvases were nearly all landscapes. Most of them were exhibited at the Academy, where "Murthly Moss" appeared in 1888; "Murthly Water," and "The Old Garden," in 1889; "The

Moon is up and yet it is not Night," in 1890; "Lingering
Autumn," and "Glen Birnam," in 1891; and "Blow, Blow,
thou winter wind!" and "Halcyon Weather," in 1892; but
he also sent his "Christmas Eve" to Mr Maclean's gallery
in 1888, and "Dew-Drenched Furze" to the New Gallery
in 1890. After 1892, however, he painted no more out-of-
door subjects, and occupied himself only with portraits and
occasional figure compositions of the type that he had
accustomed people to expect from him.

Besides his landscapes he contributed little to the
Academy between 1887 and 1891. "Murthly Moss"
was his sole picture in 1888; he had for 1889 a single
portrait, of "Mrs Paul Hardy"; and again, for 1890,
only the portrait of "The Right Hon. W. E. Gladstone
and his Grandson." But at other galleries he was fairly
well represented: by "The Last Rose of Summer" (1888),
"Forlorn" (1888), and a "Portrait of a Lady" (1890), at
the New Gallery; by portraits of "Sir Arthur Sullivan"
(1888), and "C. J. Wertheimer" (1888), and "Shelling
Peas" (1889), at the Grosvenor Gallery; and "Ducklings"
(1889), and "Afternoon Tea" (1890), at Mr Maclean's
gallery. The Academy, however, had all his work in
1891, portraits of "The Hon. Mrs Herbert Gibbs," "Mrs
Joseph Chamberlain," and "Dorothy, daughter of Mrs
Harry Lawson," as well as his two landscapes, and a
picture, "Grace." A small painting of a child, "The
Little Speedwell's Darling Blue," was there next year,
and "Sweet Emma Moreland," a young woman carrying
a basket, was at the New Gallery.

Again, in 1893, he was exhibiting only at Burlington
House, where he sent four pictures, "The Girlhood of St
Theresa," two studies of children, "Pensive," and "Merry,"
and his characteristic portrait of "John Hare," the admirable actor. Then came a gap of a year in the sequence of
his appearances, and it was not till 1895 that his next
pictures were seen. Four of these were at the Academy,

ST STEPHEN

a portrait of "Ada, Daughter of Robert Rintoul Simon, Esq.," and three compositions, "St Stephen," "A Disciple," and "Speak! Speak!" which was purchased by the Chantrey Fund Trustees, and is now in the Tate Gallery. Two others went to the New Gallery, "The Empty Cage," and "Time the Reaper," one of his few symbolical paintings, and full of pathetic suggestion as the work of an artist whose career was then rapidly drawing to its close.

What remained to him was, indeed, but a brief spell of existence. Before another spring had come round the disease from which he was suffering had made so much progress that there was little hope of prolonging his life for more than a few months. But all the more, perhaps, on this account he showed no desire to rest. The Academy of 1896 contained five pictures by him, the chief of which, "A Forerunner," illustrated rather the point of view of his early days than that of his more assured middle period. It was a reversion to the religious suggestion of the Pre-Raphaelites, though in treatment it had all the vigour of design and certainty of touch that came to him in later years. Nor did his other canvases, portraits of "Sir Richard Quain," "The Hon. John Neville Manners," "Stanley Leighton, M.P.," and "The Marchioness of Tweeddale," imply any abandonment of his splendid confidence. All that was best in his art endured to the very end; and it was never his lot to lag superfluous on the stage parodying in his decay the successes of his maturity.

CHAPTER V

WITH all his definiteness of opinion and sincere belief in the accuracy of his own judgment, it cannot be said that Sir John Millais was ever afflicted with that vice of mannerism which occasionally swamps the individuality of the industrious and prolific artist. He was too keenly alive to the varieties of nature, too earnest in his observa- tion of the life about him, to fall into the mechanical habit of repeating himself. Moreover, the bent of his mind was not in the direction of those intellectual speculations which are apt to absorb the dreamer and to warp him away from reality into fanciful conventions. He was robust, modern, and practical, a man whose instinct was active rather than contemplative; and he might even be said to be wanting in imagination, if by imagination is understood the capacity to evolve things curious and unusual out of the inner con- sciousness.

But if he lacked imagination in this sense, he more than made up for the deficiency by the exquisite acute- ness of his insight into natural facts, and by the depth of his judgment about the essentials of art. He made no mistakes through ignorance or want of proper prepara- tion; and he never failed because he grudged the preliminary thought. needed to carry to success a great undertaking. Indeed, the one thing that he always preached was application, constant industry devoted to the task of finding out how work should be done. Care- lessness he condemned; but he had no love for that type of performance which shows the trouble that the producer

CALLER HERRIN'

THE CAPTIVE

has taken over it. He contended, justly, that it was the duty of the artist to so master the executive details of his profession that his work should impress the spectator by its ready certainty rather than its conscientious toil.

This view of artistic responsibilities he expressed in an essay, " Thoughts on our Art of To-day," which appeared a few years ago in the *Magazine of Art*, and in one passage he summed up what was really his whole creed as an executant : " The commonest error into which a critic can fall is the remark we so often hear that such and such an artist's work is ' careless ' and ' would be better had more labour been spent upon it.' As often as not this is wholly untrue. As soon as the spectator can see that ' more labour has been spent upon it' he may be sure that the picture is to that extent incomplete and unfinished, while the look of freshness that is inseparable from a really successful picture would of necessity be absent. If the high finish of a picture is so apparent as immediately to force itself upon the spectator, he may know that it is not as it should be; and, from the moment that the artist feels his work is becoming a labour, he may depend upon it, it will be without freshness, and to that extent without the merit of a true work of art. Work should always look as though it had been done with ease, however elaborate ; what we see should appear to have been done without effort, whatever may be the agonies beneath the surface." And in the same essay he gave a hint of his own method : " Sometimes as I paint I may find my work becoming laborious ; but as soon as I detect any evidence of that labour I paint the whole thing out without more ado."

The need to strive for the quality of freshness, in technical expression, was, however, very far from being the only thing he insisted upon. He had, as well, a strong belief in the importance of a definitely independent attitude with regard to choice of pictorial motive, and

selection of suitable material. But beyond this he advocated special precautions against any narrowing of the
artist's practice by too close adherence to one kind of
picture. In his "Thoughts" he put this conviction into
words of considerable significance : "Individuality is not
all that should be looked to ; a varied manner must be
cultivated as well. I believe that, however admirably he
may paint in a certain method, or however perfectly he
may render a certain class of subject, the artist should
not be content to adhere to a speciality of manner or
method. A fine style is good, but it is not everything—
it is not absolutely necessary."

Certainly Sir John carried out these principles in his
own production. He had many sides to his character
as an artist, and used his powers of observation with
splendid freedom. His popularity was gained not by
the reiteration of any one set of ideas, but by showing
himself equally capable in many forms of painting. In
his figure pictures he was by turns dramatic, romantic,
sternly realistic, and at times sentimental in a robust way ;
in his portraits he was incisive, direct, and accurate ; in
his landscapes precise, exact, and searchingly correct in
his rendering of what was before him ; and in his water-
colours and drawings in black and white delightfully
facile and ingenious. He had no speciality, and no set
conviction that there was one particular thing he could
do better than anything else ; so that he never restrained
his love of variety or bound himself by limitations based
simply upon expediency.

In any classification of his works the first place must
necessarily be given to his figure-paintings and portraits.
Indeed, they make up the bulk of his achievement, and
represent the fullest growth of his capacity. The history
of his life is principally written in them. They show more
convincingly than anything else he did what manner of
man he was, and how his nature shaped itself through

DROPPED FROM THE NEST

A WAIF

many years of unremitting effort. The charm of his personality distinguishes them all—a charm as evident in the simpler and more limited subjects as in those which made great demands upon his powers of invention and contrivance. There was never any suggestion that he did not honestly feel the motive with which he was dealing, or that he was not perfectly convinced that what he had chosen was worthy of record. If he failed, it was because he had misapprehended the suitability of his material, not because he had been trying to do something outside the range of his belief.

Curiously, perhaps, his honesty and directness were at the same time the source of what was best in his pictures, and the cause of their chief weaknesses. Had he not been so frank and wholesome-minded he could never have arrived at that exquisite appreciation of the daintiness of childhood to which he gave expression in a great many of his most successful canvases, and could never have gained, as he did, the hearts of all classes of art lovers. Only a worshipper of children, with the most absolute sympathy with their ways and habits, could have painted pictures as persuasive as " Cherry Ripe," " A Waif," " Caller Herrin'," " The Princess Elizabeth," and that long series of pretty studies, of which " Perfect Bliss," " Dropped from the Nest," " Forbidden Fruit," and " Little Mrs Gamp," may be quoted as types. Only a man with the happiest sense of delicate shades of character could have commanded the extraordinary popularity that came to him as a result of his production of pictures such as these.

For instance, " Cherry Ripe," when it was issued as a coloured plate by the proprietors of *The Graphic* created a quite astonishing sensation. So great was the anxiety of the admirers of the artist to obtain this reproduction that an edition of 600,000 was exhausted in a few days, without at all satisfying the demand. Nearly

E

double the number of copies could have been sold, for the total of the orders received at *The Graphic* office approached a million. That this unprecedented success was due to the subtlety of the treatment of the picture is beyond question; the little sitter is not represented as playing a part in any drama comic or pathetic, she is placed among no romantic surroundings, and with no accessories that suggest any story. She is simply her quaint little self, perfectly child-like, absolutely natural, and without a touch of self-consciousness. She lacks the hint of stately artificiality that marks the "Souvenir of Velasquez"; she makes no appeal for sympathy, like the "Princess Elizabeth"; she is fascinating purely as a pretty piece of nature recorded by a man who was blessed with a temperament that never lost its youthful freshness.

What was a quality of inestimable value in work that lent itself well to the assertion of all that was daintiest and most refined in his conviction became now and then a source of weakness when he tried to apply it to the carrying out of more complicated themes. His drama at times descended into an artlessness that would have been feeble if it had not been redeemed by its indisputable sincerity. An example of this is afforded in "Peace Concluded, 1856," the story of which is explained · by the toy animals, taken from a Noah's ark, which are being grouped by a child upon the knee of the wounded officer who is the central figure in the picture; and there is something of the same imperfection of thought in such compositions as "The Romans leaving Britain," and "Mercy! St Bartholomew's Day." They are to be reckoned among his failures because in interpreting them he has been satisfied to be obvious and matter-of-fact, and has not risen to the greater possibilities presented by exacting subjects; just as in his "Joan of Arc" he has missed the romantic side of his heroine,

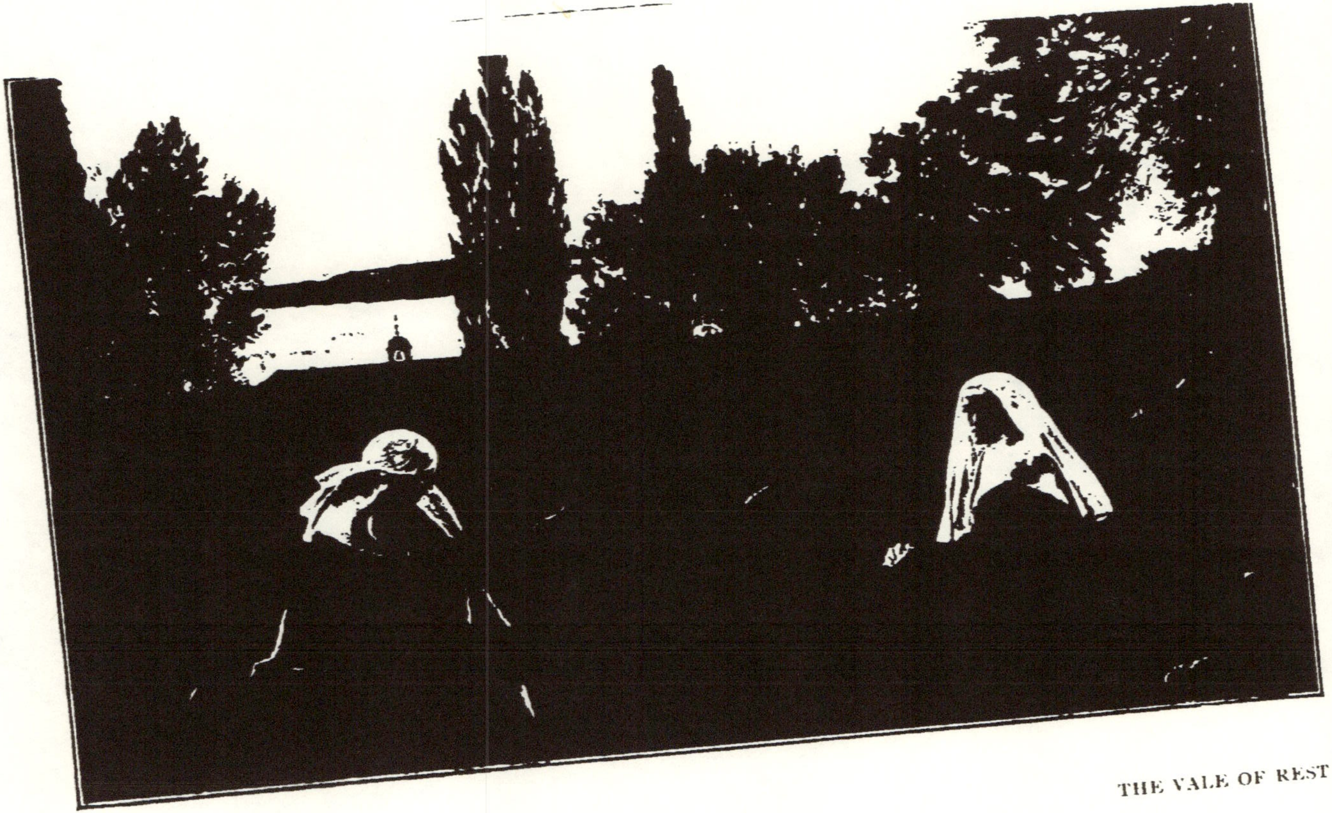

THE VALE OF REST

MERCY—ST BARTHOLOMEW'S DAY

and has made her merely an ordinary young woman in fancy dress.

Yet there are many of his canvases which prove that he had a very sound judgment of dramatic necessities, and that he could reach the greater heights of subject-painting. He has left on record his opinion that "the best painter that ever lived never entirely succeeded more than four or five times; that is to say, no artist ever painted more than four or five masterpieces, however high his general average may have been; for such success depends upon the coincidence, not only of genius and inspiration, but of health and mood and a hundred other mysterious contingencies." Applying this dictum to his own practice, it can certainly be said that he enjoyed this coincidence in full measure, and that the four or five great occasions came to him as they have to other masters. Indeed, it would be difficult to limit his masterpieces so narrowly, especially if the whole range of his production is taken into account.

Among his subject-pictures, at all events, there are quite half-a-dozen, which, by their wonderful vitality, their deep significance, and force of expression, make good a claim to the possession of the finest kind of mastery. "The Vale of Rest," "The North-West Passage," "The Order of Release," "The Ruling Passion," "The Boyhood of Raleigh," and perhaps "Effie Deans," are all canvases in which the "mysterious contingencies" have been in perfect agreement. They show that he could grasp with all possible firmness, and state with unflinching decision, motives that called for great mental exertion. Their qualities are those that come from a minute insight, not only into details of character, but also into the principles which govern the dramatic side of pictorial art. No false note spoils the harmony of these compositions, no touch of uncertainty or divided opinion; they are confident and assured, and their mean-

ing is not to be questioned. They express the thou
of a man who, with all his straightforwardness
simplicity, could now and then look beneath the su
and work out problems far more profound than it
his every-day habit to investigate.

Even in his less monumental works, in those with v
he made up his high general average, he could sh
sterling sense of artistic responsibility. Indeed, wha
chose to do was done, as a rule, with so much consist
and so much logic that the result rarely suggested
inquiry as to the sufficiency of the motive. How
slight the amount of his inspiration, the picture he
duced was usually satisfying, and, within its limita
admirably complete. It might not cause any dee
flection; it might, like "Cherry Ripe," "The Cap
"Cinderella," and many others of the same class, ai
nothing more than the reproduction of a personality;
might have only a thread of story binding togethe
various actors in the scene represented. But it was h
ever to be passed by without attention or to be disrega
as the performance of an artist who had not solidly
vinced himself before he offered to other people the p
of his mental application.

His romance, especially, had this merit of being
thought out. It was never complicated by exce
details, and was strict in its adherence to the main
of the story, without irrelevant matter introduced to
plete picturesquely an imperfect conception. "The K
Errant" is a very good example of his method of de
with an incident evolved from his own fancy; and "Vi
O Lord!" is equally characteristic as an instance o
power with which he could seize upon the salient poi
a subject suggested to him by written history. Ma
his finer paintings were illustrative, records of the im
sions made upon him by things he had read, and ex
sions of the instinct that brought him throughou

THE ESCAPE OF A HERETIC

VICTORY, O LORD

life such success as a draughtsman in black and white;
but they were only occasionally direct illustrations of
particular passages from books.   More often what he
gave was his view of what might have happened, rather
than a plain reproduction in paint of what was already
fixed in words.

He preferred to base himself more upon the spirit than
the letter of a story, to find a new reading for himself, and
to treat it with a considerable degree of independence.
In " The Princes in the Tower " he followed none of the
accepted versions, and in " Effie Deans " he made a subject
out of the slightest possible suggestion in the text of the
romance ; yet both pictures show that peculiar air of conviction which results from a perfect understanding of what
is essential for the proper application of dramatic material.
In these, as in almost all his renderings of incident, appears
his habit of attacking not the climax of the story, but
rather one of its earlier stages, an intermediate moment
when the action is still in progress and the final result is
suggested rather than clearly foreshadowed.   This habit
was always strong upon him.   It gave their particular
interest to such early works as " The Huguenot," " The
Black Brunswicker," " The · Proscribed Royalist," and
" The Escape of a Heretic," just as much as it did to
later pictures like " The Girlhood of St Theresa," or
" Speak! Speak!"; and by introducing a touch of speculation into the record of his thoughts he enhanced the
fascination which was never wanting in his sturdy in-
ventions.

Indeed, there was in every branch of his figure-painting
some sufficient reason for his popularity, some distinct
attractiveness of mental quality to add convincingly to
the impression created by his superlative command over
technicalities.   He could be tender, dainty, and refined
in his studies of children ; serious and solemn in his
symbolical compositions ; pathetic, vigorous, and passion-

atc by turns in his subject-pictures; and through all ran a vein of sentiment that was always wholesome, clean, and intelligible. He never affected to be influenced by feelings that were not honestly natural to him, nor did he pretend to represent anything that he did not believe in sincerely and without question. What he painted was invariably what he felt at the moment; and, whether it was a masterpiece, like "The North-West Passage," or a comparative failure, like "Peace Concluded," it expressed simply the appeal that the subject had made to him; and his response to this appeal was always unconventional and definite.

He trusted in the same way to a personal impression of his sitter when he set himself to paint a portrait. He had no desire to be either coarsely material or unduly fanciful in his representation of modern humanity, and he had no fixed manner of treating all sorts of types. There was in this most important section of his art no pretence that he wished to create anything, or even to build up a tradition as to the way in which the human subject should be rendered. What he wanted was to show that he understood the individuality of the man or woman before him, and that his understanding had helped him to make clear to others the special idiosyncrasies that separated that man or woman from the ordinary crowd. Portraiture to him was a matter of observation, of receptiveness to suggestion, and acceptance of what was visible, rather than an artistic process which enabled him to give free scope to his inventive instincts.

This view of his responsibilities was partly the outcome of his temperament, partly a result of the strict self-education that he had gone through in his younger days. To imitate what he had closely examined, and to state plainly what he had decided to be right, had become the main principles of his practice, and nowhere did they control him so stringently as in his portraits. But they operated

THE RIGHT HON.
W. E. GLADSTONE

chiefly in enabling him to differentiate between the many personalities that during the latter half of his life were presented to him for pictorial record. His likenesses were always vitally exact, and each one had the power to claim attention by its vivid reproduction of the living subject. Yet they were never wanting in distinctive quality of style, and never verged upon the flippant familiarity which is the vice of certain modern schools. Dignity, perhaps in some instances coldness, of aspect is a feature of his canvases. No picturesque attitudes, no appeal to the onlooker, no smiling self-advertisement, were permitted to the people he represented. They were made to live by the magic of his brush, but they had to live up to his high ideal of behaviour, and to comport themselves with proper restraint.

It is very interesting to see how he managed to secure invariably this atmosphere of distinction without losing either individuality or subtlety of characterisation. Facial expression of the most obvious sort he did not attempt. He painted the features preferably in repose, unaltered by any emotion, and moved by nothing in the nature of momentary thought. This normal composure, however, was not stolid quiescence, the somnolent blankness that obliterates character and hides the feelings behind a mask ; it was the restfulness of the active and intelligent mind, reserved and reflective in the intervals between moments of intellectual exertion. It suggested the quiet dignity of habitual impartiality, and by its freedom from particular assertion summarised with comprehensive truth all the nobler attributes of the person depicted.

That this preference for repose in representation did not lead the artist into a dry convention, or into any disregard of the essential points of difference between people, is very evident if a comparison is made of his chief portraits. Beneath their reserve appears a wonderful variety of manner, and a superb power of

interpretation.   They are studied, exact, and intens
real, records of acute analysis applied with thorough
crimination, and of masterly mechanism used with
control.   No perfunctory labour appears in them,
their value is diminished by no slurring over of
little things which help to define the more intin
characteristics of the modern man.

As a study in subtleties it is instructive to exan
such a portrait as that of Mr John Hare, and to i
with what skill the mobile features of the nerv
animated face are rendered, and how the vivacit}
the actor is suggested by refinement of modelling
sensitiveness of drawing.   There is, too, a valu
illustration of Sir John's methods to be obtained
comparing with this portrait another of an equ
eminent member of the same profession.   Facially t
is little in common between Mr Hare and Sir H(
Irving, but the artist in painting them has made
difference not merely one of feature.   He has ma
accurately and with perfect comprehension the diverg(
between the exquisite manipulator of dramatic detail
rejoices in high finish and infinite exactness of impers(
tion, and the deep thinker whose life has been devote
the working out of those great artistic problems which
modern theatre manager has to face.

Another instance of his faculty for realising the me
character of his sitter is afforded by the marvellous p(
of the 1885 portrait of Mr Gladstone, a suprer
accomplished record of a complex personality in w
were blended indomitable will, militant energy,
stern decision, with a strain of almost fanatical entl
asm and credulity.   To contrast with it the sphinx
and inscrutable head of Lord Salisbury, the tender dre
and poetic face of Mr Hook, with the artistic temperar
proclaimed in every line, the "Thomas Carlyle," so
and cynical, and at war with existence, or the sad, w

THE MOST HON.
THE MARQUESS OF SALISBURY,

MR JOHN HARE

and wearied features of Lord Beaconsfield, painted during the last days of that statesman's life, is to review the whole range of possibilities that were grasped by an artist who was endowed with insight such as only the greatest masters can be said to possess, and with a responsiveness of hand to eye that was well-nigh perfect.

Perhaps he was less analytical and less discriminating in his pictures of women. They seemed to appeal to him less than men did as subjects for psychological study. What he preferred to dwell upon were the physical charms of femininity, beauty of face and form, elegance of carriage, and that rounded fulness of development that argues perfect wholesomeness of body and mind. The stateliness of the card-players in " Hearts are Trumps," the air of high breeding and conscious power which distinguishes the portrait of the Duchess of Westminster, and the more matronly splendour of " Mrs Bischoffsheim," mark the chief variations in his manner of painting womankind ; occasionally only did he diverge into more detailed character, as in " Miss Eveleen Tennant," " Mrs Jopling," and " Mrs Perugini " ; but as a rule he was content to treat the freshness and brilliant vitality of his feminine sitters, and to leave untouched their possibilities of passion or strong emotion. His men were full of vigorous aspirations, restrained for the moment yet near the surface and ready at any moment to break into activity ; but his women were serene and unmoved, prepared, perhaps, for conquest, but wrapped in a reserve that would not allow them to make the first advances.

It is curious that, in his portrait of himself, he should have departed to some extent from his usual habit with regard to the masculine sitter, and should have been comparatively unobservant of his own character. He painted himself with a certain degree of idealisation, minimising the physical force which was the great attraction of his face, and attempting a kind of dreamy abstraction that was

scarcely true. It may be that he wished to expres
view of himself which he put into words with regard
picture of him that Frank Holl produced in 1886.
comment made by Millais on this work was, "I k
look a bit of a farmer ; but then I am also a bit of
And Holl has made me all farmer and no poet."
Uffizi Gallery portrait is certainly that of a poet, ᵻ
contemplative, and without much hint of that sᵽ
tenacity which made Millais so striking a figure
record of the British School. Still, even if it sᵢ
suggests the man we knew, it is by its very unlikeɪ
the general run of his portraits specially interestin
revelation of his estimate of himself; and as a p
painting it is notably important.

About his technical methods there is compar
little to be said. He was not a worker who con
himself very deeply over devices of execution, or cᵢ
codify his system of painting in accordance with sc
principles. He drew well, and handled his materia
the sureness and confidence that came from complete
ledge of what he wanted to do. His chief desire,
been already stated, was to retain in pictures th
really cost him deep thought and prolonged labᵢ
aspect of spontaneity and freshness ; to be direct iɪ
ment and simple in expression. He had a well-fᵢ
belief that the finest art was that in which the mea
the artist was to be realised with the least amo
seeking and with as little inquiry as possible abᵢ
intentions. Consequently, he strove all his life to
the intricacies of his craft, so that no hesitation on ƕ
might make his meaning vague or indefinite. Sᵽ
always had. ·Even in the apparently laborious perioᵢ
Pre-Raphaelite performance he could, and did, paɪ
amazing facility—the head of Ferdinand, in "Feɪ
lured by Ariel," was, for instance, completed in fivᵢ
—and as years went on his certainty became eveɪ

MRS JOPLING

indisputable. "Cherry Ripe" was painted in a week, "The Last Rose of Summer" in not more than four days, and for many of his portraits half-a-dozen sittings sufficed to give him all that was necessary for the achievement of a masterpiece. His quickness of apprehension and accuracy of vision helped him to a prompt decision as to choice of material; and when his direction was once fixed, his inexhaustible energy carried him easily through the work of production. Nature had well equipped him for his profession, and wisely he followed the lines she had laid down.

CHAPTER VI

W HAT is exactly the estimate that can be formed o
value of the contributions made by Sir John Milla
the landscape art of this century depends, to a very
siderable extent, upon the view that the inquirer may
concerning the manner in which out-of-door suk
should be attacked. Landscape painting is large
matter of personal feeling, and is far less than any (
form of artistic practice amenable to rules and re;
tions. The particular individuality of the painter
special preferences and susceptibilities, play the chief
both in his choice of material and in his decision :
the shaping of it upon canvas; and the willingne
art lovers to accept his statements without reservati(
question is greatly affected by the impressionabili1
these observers to nature's suggestions. Many p(
have unconsciously strong convictions about the as
of the world about them, convictions based not
reason, but arising rather from association and habi1
they happen to find in any painter a kindred spirit
thinks and sees as they do, they are apt to exalt
often unduly, simply because they understand wha
has to say; and they are inclined to underrate the
equally convinced, ˙whose instincts have led him
different direction.

The unquestionable popularity that Millais gaine
his excursions into landscape was certainly due t(
fact that his observation was of the ordinary and e
day kind. He was a student of nature, not an imagin

interpreter of what she presented. He dealt with facts and left fancies almost entirely alone. In the series of canvases that began with "Chill October" and ended with "Halcyon Weather" there was infinite industry, marvellous accuracy, perfect veracity of record, but little effort to be anything but absolutely exact in his statement of what he saw. He proved completely the dictum of Mr Ruskin, quoted at length in the first chapter, that he "sees everything, small and large, with almost the same clearness; mountains and grasshoppers alike; the leaves on the branches; the veins in the pebbles, the bubbles in the stream; but he can remember nothing and invent nothing. Patiently he sets himself to his mighty task; abandoning at once all thoughts of seizing transient effects, or giving general impressions of that which his eyes present to him in microscopical dissection, he chooses some small portion out of the infinite scene, and calculates with courage the number of weeks which must elapse before he can do justice to the intensity of his perceptions, or the fulness of matter in his subject."

But this love of "microscopical dissection" is exactly that which is strongest in the ordinary man. To admire the subtle poetry of Corot, the splendid dignity of Constable, or the illimitable imagination of Turner, is given to few minds, and implies either the possession of special faculties or the development of an exceptional taste. The general run of mankind cares little about intellectual abstractions, and prefers what is clear and tangible. So the artist who paints realities with power and decision is surer of wide acceptance than he who dreams exquisitely and records his dreams with fastidious refinement. He finds many people who neither understand nor appreciate the glories of infinite space, people with imagination insufficient to build mental images upon suggestions from which detail is eliminated, and in which nothing is offered but great fundamental principles; and

if his own inclinations lie in the direction of analysi
little things rather than comprehension of the whole
which they form part, he soon discovers that by gi\
way to his instincts he can secure an amount of appro
that would never be within his reach if he strove to enl
his scope and acquire that wider view which could com
him only by a strenuous process of special self-educatic

It cannot be said that Millais ever did make this e
to extend the limits of his observation of nature ; it r
indeed, be doubted whether he even felt the necessity
it. His conviction was so strong, and his excusable (
fidence in his own judgment was so complete, that t]
was probably in his mind no hesitation about follov
a congenial course. Moreover, it is easy to believe '
the acclamation with which his first essays in pure la
scape were received confirmed him in the resolve to p
what was obviously to the taste of a considerable sec
of the public. There was no question then of fighting
recognition against an almost overpowering weigh
opposition. He had, before 1871, when "Chill Octol
appeared, won his way to the front rank of pop
favourites, and any new effort he made was sure of b
treated with respect. He had proved that his capa
was great enough to justify a general faith in the v
of his artistic achievement, and that his new depart
would probably be not less significant and authorita
than those more familiar attempts by which his reputa
had been established.

Certainly, if the rather futile speculation as to wha
might have done in landscape, if his temperament
been other than it was, is abandoned, it must be admi
that within his limitations he was extraordinarily able.
amazing patience and his surprising quickness of vi:
enabled him to grasp with absolute accuracy the plain f
of nature, and his command of brushwork ensured a
perfection in his pictorial expression of the matter that

THE BLIND GIRL

had selected for representation. When he chose a "small portion out of the infinite scene," as the subject for his picture, he had no idea of evading difficulties, nor had he any intention of avoiding that responsibility as an artist, the acceptance of which was the controlling principle of his life. In landscape, he was as minutely attentive, as surely certain of himself, as he ever was in his figure work. Nothing was implied, or left in sketchy incompleteness, because his patience had failed him before he had realised the complicated fulness of his subject. He spared himself no toil to arrive at what seemed to him to be the perfection of nature, and his courage was proof against every demand.

As a necessary consequence, however, of this manner of working, he never could be ranked among the inspired painters of the open air, nor could he ever be said to have dealt exhaustively with the problems presented by natural phenomena. He remained untouched by the subtleties of atmospheric effect, by the varieties of momentary illumination, or by the fleeting glories of aërial colour, which provide the student of nature's devices with the chief incentive to artistic effort. He was always too much concerned with the things at his feet, with matter that he could dissect and investigate, to give much thought to the broad and comprehensive scheme of which these things formed part. Whatever he arrived at in the way of a record of a natural effect was reached, not so much by thorough understanding of the effect as a whole, as by an amazingly acute interpretation of the influence exercised by it upon the details upon which his eyes were fixed.

An excellent instance of this is afforded in " The Blind Girl," where he has given little enough attention to the grandeur of the passing storm-clouds, and has concentrated the whole of his energies upon the rendering, with supreme fidelity, of dripping weeds and a drenched hill-side, lighted

by the rays of the setting sun. As a record of microscop
insight, the picture is superlatively successful; it cou
hardly be more exact, or more closely reasoned out; b
as a representation of Nature in one of her most impre
sive moods, it is ineffectual and unconvincing. So, too, I
most popular landscape, "Chill October," falls short
greatness, because it is too plainly studied bit by bit, a
part by part, and built up precisely by the careful putti
in place of material collected for the pictorial purpose.
holds together, not because it has one great dominati
intention, but because its construction is so ingenious, a
its mechanism so workmanlike, that no single detail c
be criticised as out of relation to the rest. It can hard
be called learned in design, nor can it be said to have a
conspicuous dignity of style; yet the knowledge of for
the intimate observation of the growth of riversi
vegetation, and the appreciation of autumnal colouri
which were turned to account by the artist in his treatme
of the subject, make the canvas prominent among t
greatest nature studies of modern times. In its particu
qualities of truth and industry, it is, indeed, so notal
that there is no difficulty in accepting it as a piece of ra
accomplishment, beyond all comparison with what otr
painters have attempted in the same direction.

There is in existence a note written in 1882 by t
artist—it is pasted on to the back of the canvas—which
not only an explanation of the method pursued by him
painting this picture, but also gives an idea of the spirit
which he attacked all his work in the open air. "'Ch
October' was painted from a backwater of the Tay ju
below Kinfauns, near Perth. The scene, simple as it
had impressed me for years before I painted it. T
traveller between Perth and Dundee passes the spot whe
I stood. Danger on either side—the tide, which or
carried away my platform, and the trains which threaten
to blow my work into the river. I chose the subject for t

sentiment it always conveyed to my mind, and I am happy
to think that the transcript touched the public in a like
manner, although many of my friends at the time were at
a loss to understand what I saw to paint in such a scene.
I made no sketch for it, but painted every touch from
nature, on the canvas itself, under irritating trials of wind
and rain. The only studio-work was in connection with
the effect."

This, indeed, expresses the whole of his point of view
with reference to the choice and treatment of the material
which he selected for his landscapes. The sentiment of
the scene appealed to him in the first place, and induced
him to fix upon this or that particular subject; but when
he had decided that the subject was worthy of attention
his anxiety was to reproduce it in absolute portraiture, to
put in everything that with the closest search he could
discover, and to leave out none of the little details that the
intensity of his perceptions enabled him to detect. It was
an enlargement of the same idea that governed him in his
Pre-Raphaelite days, when he painted every leaf in the
background of the "Ophelia," the tangle of the woodland
undergrowth in the " Proscribed Royalist," or the weather
stains and the little patches of moss and lichen on the
wall against which his figures were set in the " Huguenot ";
a development of that sincere love of realism on which his
artistic creed was based. Beyond the limits of actuality
he never strayed ; and at their worst his landscapes had a
tendency to show a little too plainly how little of genuine
inspiration entered into their composition.

One consequence of his habit of reflecting simply what
he could keep before him for the period necessary for the
painstaking working out of his canvases, was that he rarely
depicted any other season of the year than autumn or
early winter. At other times he was busy in his London
studio, too fully occupied to spare the days or weeks that
he required for painting a landscape as he held it should

F

be painted. Almost his only representation of the s
was seen in "Apple Blossoms," which belongs to a
before his powers as a portrait painter had been recog
and before the demands made upon him by a succe
of sitters had limited his opportunities for country e
sions. During the latter half of his life, however, he
a practice of spending the autumn months in Scotland
it was there that he was able to give way to that lc
nature which was so strong in him—as he once expi
it : "I do so delight in painting landscapes, so much
than portraiture ! . . . . You can so completely j
yourself in landscape : you have only yourse
satisfy."

To these autumns in Scotland was due the prodi
of such canvases as "Flowing to the River," "Flowi
the Sea," and "The Sound of Many Waters," all p
on the Tay or its tributaries ; "Scotch Firs," "V
Fuel," "Murthly Moss," "Murthly Water," and "Urc
Castle" ; and "Over the Hills and Far Away," "Th
Garden," and "The Fringe of the Moor," in each of
is seen the most ample evidence of his enthusiastic
and of his marvellous accuracy in the rendering (
results of certain conditions of weather and of the ch
produced in the face of the country by the march (
seasons. Only here and there in the whole series
landscapes can one be noted which hints at any des
emphasise the impression made upon him by some p
subtlety of atmosphere, or by some momentary cha
effect ; and only occasionally can he be said to have re
to the poetry which was so definitely felt in such (
pictures as "Autumn Leaves," "Sir Isumbras," or
Vale of Rest.". In "The Old Garden," he treated a
and appreciatively the quiet stillness of autumn tw
the repose of evening in those later months of the
when the first touches of winter frost give warning (
rigours to come ; and in "The Moon is up and ye

not Night," he found a similar motive worthy of earnest analysis.

Perhaps the deepest feeling of which he was capable appeared in the few pictures that he painted of actual winter. In his renderings of snow he displayed a degree of vigour that was peculiarly dramatic and admirably in keeping with the storm and stress of the winter season. Unluckily, this particular aspect of nature was one that he rarely attempted. In his "Mistletoe Gatherer," produced in 1884, he made his first experiment in this direction ; but he is said to have had doubts, on technical grounds, whether white pigments would have sufficient permanency to justify their almost exclusive use in a large picture, and so he did not repeat the experiment until four years later when these doubts had been removed by the testimony of a number of his professional brethren. Then he painted "Christmas Eve," a view of Murthly Castle by sunset with snow lying deep upon its terraces ; and followed, in 1891, with "Glen Birnam," an admirably designed and powerfully expressed winter landscape ; and, in 1892, with "Blow, blow, thou Winter Wind," one of the most convincing statements of the turmoil of a biting December gale that modern art can show.

But still, even if it is possible to select from among the landscapes which Millais painted a few that express the more profound and abstract meanings of nature, the majority of them must be reckoned rather as astonishingly vivid representations of her superficial features than as inspirations based upon the suggestions with which she is so lavish. They belong to what Mr Ruskin called the Natural History class, when, in his 1875 *Academy Notes*, he somewhat fiercely attacked "The Fringe of the Moor," and their most evident merit is their unflinching naturalism. How far their truth can be described, in the words of the great critic, as "essential, though rude and apparently motiveless veracity," it is not quite easy to say ; their

exact position among the pictures of this century mu
always be a matter of opinion. It is possible, from o
standpoint, to deny to them any of the spirit by whi
landscape in the largest sense should be dignified, and it
equally possible to go to the other extreme and to h
them as revelations of all that is most learned a
exhaustive in the way of nature study ; the attitude of t
observer must necessarily depend almost entirely upon t
way in which nature appeals to him, and upon whate·
preference he may have for one manner of treatment o·
another.

At least there cannot be argued against the artist tl
his landscape art lacked in the smallest degree eit.
knowledge or industry. His comment on his pract
—" I have often been laboured, but, whatever I ₁
I am never careless"—applies as fully to his out-of-d
work as to his figure-pictures. No one but a devo
and scientific craftsman could have painted so exa(
the swirl and movement of water as he has done in
Flood," or " The Sound of Many Waters," or could h
given so perfectly the character of living vegetation as
has in the foreground of " Chill October," and in the le
fringe that overhangs the pool in " Halcyon Weathe
and only a draughtsman of infinite conscience could h
suggested with such absolute economy of labour the ext
of aërial space which is so fascinating in his drawing
" Orley Farm." These things prove that landscape ·
not with him a recreation, the occupation of his leis
moments when he wished to lay aside the weigh
responsibilities of his profession and amuse himself v
something slighter and less absorbing. He only alte
his focus when he got out-of-doors ; there was no cha
in the minuteness of his observation.

If anything in the way of attempted definition
desirable, it may perhaps be said of him that he looke(
open-air nature with the eyes of the portrait painter, ₁

A FLOOD

By permission of Arthur Lucas,
publisher of the large Mezzotint Engraving

studied her features as he did those of the sitter posed
before him in his studio. He searched her face for the
little lines and modellings by which her character was
marked, and he considered every detail that seemed to
him to define her personality. He concentrated himself,
in fact, chiefly upon the small things, and forgot meanwhile
to note the largeness of the general scheme in which these
trifles played but minor parts. But his concentration was
without pedantry, and his love of detail without pettiness.
Both were essential elements in his organisation, and they
were inspired by that single-minded simplicity which was
at all times his most persuasive attribute.

CHAPTER VII

IT has been well said that if Millais had never dev
himself to the painting of oil pictures, but had g
his life entirely to the work of book illustration,
position among the chief leaders of the British Sc
would still have been indisputable, and his magnifi
ability would have been amply demonstrated. Ther
indeed, a great deal of truth in this contention. Althc
the world would have been the poorer for the loss o:
masterly essays in brushwork, and of his wonderful e
cises in the arrangement of strong colour, it would 1
possessed extremely significant evidence of the realit
his artistic judgment, and of the adaptability of his
ventive powers. In his black and white work he shc
frequently a side of his capacity that appeared in his p:
ing only on great occasions, a sense of dramatic exigen
a feeling for illustrative meanings, far beyond what
suggested by the general run of his pictures. A:
interpreter of the fancies of other men he was exceptioi
intelligent, with a memorable grasp of the salient p(
of the story and a remarkable facility in summari
essentials. He was afraid of nothing in the way
subject, and spared no labour to make his draw
completely expressive.

His love of black and white was indeed a gen
one. Illustration was not to him, as it so often is
other men, a mere expedient, resorted to because
unappreciative public refused to recognise the merit
importance of his paintings, and abandoned gladl'

From Tennyson's Poems 1857   THE SISTERS

soon as he found he could make a sufficient income without it.   On the contrary, he welcomed the opportunities with which this branch of art practice provided him, and regarded them as of the highest value. For more than twenty years he was a prolific illustrator, constantly busy with drawings that were reproduced in all kinds of books and magazines ; and even in his later life occasional examples appeared to prove that his hand had not lost its cunning and that his interest in this type of work was undiminished.

How deeply he felt about this particular subject is, perhaps, best proved by his constant advocacy, within and without the Academy, of the claims of illustrative draughtsmen to official recognition.   Before the Royal Commission on the Academy he strenuously urged that workers in black and white should be declared eligible for election to membership of that institution as draughtsmen purely, instead of being required to disguise themselves as picture painters before they could hope for admission ; and his pleading then expressed a conviction which remained strong in him till his death.   Mr Spielmann, in his book, "Millais and his Works," quotes a remark made by the artist, as President of the Academy, that if he had lived he would have done his utmost to persuade his fellow-members at Burlington House to adopt his view and to enlarge the narrow Academic borders so as to include the followers of a branch of art which is without an equal in its hold on the public, and of the greatest importance as a means of encouraging a true taste in æsthetics.   He spoke with real authority on a matter that, both by inclination and association, he was fully qualified to discuss.   His experience of illustrative drawing, and his acquaintance with the history of its development, were both peculiarly intimate ; and he knew exactly what were the possibilities of influence possessed by the craft.

Indeed, it may fairly be argued that he
influential in laying the foundations of the g
school of illustrators than he was in leading
renascence of pictorial effort which has, in le
a-century, raised British art from a moribun
condition of vitality that has hardly been equ
previous epoch in its history. Among the
of the sixties, among the men whom preser
place in the front rank of the world's work
and white, Millais stands out as the acknow
He was as plainly their champion, as he was
ating and militant spirit of the Pre-Rapha
always the first in every movement that
increase the opportunities open to the artists (
the conditions under which their productic
presented to the public. It was largely in
his demand that those changes were made ir
of wood engraving by which drawing on th
freed from undesirable limitations, and the
under which illustrators had previously s
removed ; so that, indirectly, he may be s
created the facilities which were enjoyed by
draughtsmen who followed in his footsteps.

The company which he led between 1850
the force both of example and precept, was
brilliancy. It included not only his own im
temporaries and friends, Holman Hunt, and
many younger men, who year by year attache
to it and carried on, each in his own way, t
of working which Millais convincingly ext
complete list would comprise an extraordina
names that are. familiar to every student of
Fred Walker, Pinwell, Houghton, J. W. N
Charles Keene, Du Maurier, Poynter, to quo
of the most prominent, and would serve wel
of a great revival. That he should have kep

From Tennyson's Poems 1857   LOCKSLEY HALL

From Tennyson's Poems 1857   DEATH OF THE OLD YEAR

the head of them all, not simply by virtue of his seniority, but essentially by his indisputable power, both of hand and mind, is one of the most emphatic pieces of evidence that could be adduced to prove the importance of his intervention in illustrative art.   It justifies absolutely, if any justification were necessary, the present estimate of his superiority over the greater number of the draughtsmen of this century.

Very early in his life Millais showed signs of that capacity to express much with a few happy touches, which was constantly exemplified in the long series of his drawings for reproduction.   Even as a child his random sketches were full of character, and yet direct and easy in their manner of expression ; and, as he grew up, and gained more and more command over methods, he amplified the significance of his style without losing any of its straightforward directness.   Knowledge of technical refinements freed his hand and opened up to him wider possibilities of expression, but it did not lead him to make any kind of display of mere cleverness at the expense of the nobler qualities of design.   The idea by which he was always controlled was to strive for fidelity of interpretation, for that manner of treating his subject which would put its point beyond all doubt, and leave no room for dispute about the meaning of the incident chosen for illustration.   He attempted no assertion of his own special preferences for any particular pictorial manner, but kept himself in harmony with the story that he had to handle, and put the resources of his art frankly at the disposal of the writer whose word-pictures he had to render in black and white.

As an example of his adaptability, even at the outset of his career as an artist, the drawing of "The Battle of Stirling," which belongs to Lady Dilke, is worth attention. Its extraordinary vivacity and strength, both of composition and draughtsmanship, would seem to be the outcome of careful preparation and prolonged thought ; and yet the history of its production proves it to have been a piece of momentary inspiration, an illustration of a subject suddenly suggested and carried out on the spot. The date of the drawing is about 1849, when Millais was staying at Shotover House making studies for his picture of "Ferdinand and Ariel." One evening he was amusing a party of children, of whom Lady Dilke was one, by sketching various subjects that they chose ; and it was in response to a request from her for an illustration of the Battle of Stirling that this drawing was executed. A moment's consideration, and a glance at a book of military costumes, which was beside him on the table, sufficed by way of preparation, and the sketch, with all its vigorous movement and happy suggestion of the turmoil of battle, was promptly completed and handed over to the child, who carried it home in triumph.

To these early years, when the Pre-Raphaelite movement was in the first flush of its enthusiastic activity, belong many wonderful drawings full of minute detail and conceived with infinite ingenuity, careful compositions recording subjects chosen from history or from the poems and romances to which he devoted constant study. The methods of execution followed by the artist in making these designs were very varied. Sometimes he used pencil, sometimes pen and ink, but not infrequently he chose as his medium ink applied with a brush, as in his "Spoliation of the Tomb of Queen Matilda," or pen and ink with washes of colour, as in his exquisite drawing of "St Agnes," illustrating Tennyson's poem "St Agnes' Eve." Occasionally he expressed himself through the process of etching, but of his work in this direction there are extant very few instances, and these, it seems, must be assigned entirely to the period when the views of the Brotherhood influenced him and led him into experiments which he did not follow up in later life. In water-colour, however, he painted constantly. Many of his more important pictures were worked out in this medium before he commenced them upon

From Tennyson's Poems 1857   ST AGNES' EVE

From Tennyson' Poems 1857

EDWARD GRAY AND
EMMA MORELAND

canvas; and, besides, he has left a number of other water-
colours which were not intended as studies to be developed
later on, but were independent examples of his use of a
particular form of technical practice that gave him excellent
results.

The first conspicuous assertion of his power as an illustrator was given in 1857, when Edward Moxon published
the quarto edition of Tennyson's poems.   With Holman
Hunt, Rossetti, and several other young artists, Millais was
chosen to make drawings for the book, and the manner in
which he turned to account the special opportunities presented by the material which he found then at his disposal,
confirmed at once the good opinion that the more judicious
observers had formed about his chances of success in this
branch of art.   He stamped himself as an instinctive
translator, with the acutest perception of the pictorial
possibilities of the text that was put before him, and a
marvellous faculty for keeping sympathetically in touch
with the intentions of the author.   His imagination, it
must be remembered, was not of the erratic order, prone
to build strange fancies upon an insufficient foundation,
and ready to lead him into speculations only vaguely connected with the original matter he had undertaken to study.
His natural equipment for his work was something much
better than that, for what he had instead was the far more
valuable quality of intelligence.   Rarely enough did he
miss the true signification of the passage he had to illus-
rate, and still more rarely did he fail to make his explanation of it completely graphic and decisive.

To say that he took his colour from the writer with
whom he was associated is not to imply any disparagement of his ability.   Rather it may be taken as an acknowledgment of his fitness for his work.   If he had been less
tractable, or less inclined to use his analytical skill for the
dissection of the ideas formed by the literary craftsman, he
would never have shown that astonishing variety and

versatility by which he was distinguished, and certainly he
would never have touched those depths of knowledge
and thought which he sounded time after time with perfect confidence. It was this sense of adaptation, and
this capacity for assimilating knowledge, that made his
Tennyson drawings so impressive. In such designs as the
" Mariana," " St Agnes' Eve," " The Sisters," and the
" Death of the Old Year," and in the slighter " Locksley
Hall," and " Edward Gray and Emma Moreland," it is the
very mind of the poet that is pictured, and every touch set
down by the artist aims at conveying to the observer
exactly and faithfully the mental picture that the words
suggest. The illustrations give us nothing that is not
already enshrined in the text, nor do they hint at any
novel or unexpected reading of its hidden meanings ; they
may be said to make it visible, and to put the poetic
imagery into a tangible form.

These Tennyson drawings were, however, but a foretaste
of a feast of work of the same class provided lavishly by
Millais during the decade that followed. In 1859 " Once a
Week " was started, and he began with the first volume a
connection with that magazine that continued without
interruption for some years. Among the earlier drawings
that he contributed to its pages were illustrations to the
lines by Tom Taylor on " Magenta " and " The Plague of
Elliant," and among those that followed in rapid succession
were " Farmer Chell's Kitchen," " Margaret Wilson," " The
Monk," " A Fair Jacobite," which he afterwards painted as
" The White Cockade," and " The Mite of Dorcas," which
was the germ of the idea later on elaborated as " The
Widow's Mite." Most of these were comparatively slight
in handling, bearing evidences of speed in execution, and
treated with straightforward and ready simplicity ; but in
scarcely a single instance do they show any failure to
appreciate correctly and vividly the subject-matter selected.

During the same period he completed a set of nineteen

THE HIDDEN TREASURE

THE WICKED HUSBANDMAN

signs of quite a different character, carefully reasoned
t and minutely detailed drawings of "The Parables of
ır Lord." These appeared first as magazine illustrations,
Good Words, a periodical to which he was a frequent
ntributor; but about 1864 they were issued as a volume
· Messrs Routledge. The series shows a certain continu-
s evolution in his technical methods, a progress from
e closeness of application by which the black and white
his Pre-Raphaelite days was marked to the freedom of
uch and largeness of style that belong to his drawings
ring the later sixties. It is interesting in this connec-
ın to compare the minuteness of "The Hidden Treasure,"
"The Unmerciful Servant," with the more suggestive
ɔseness of handling in "The Wicked Husbandman," or
Che Tares"; for by this comparison may be realised
uch of the innate inclination of his mind, and a
fficiently clear insight may be obtained into the nature
 those changes by which the course of his practice, not
ıly in black and white, but in painting as well, was
:termined.

For the highest manifestation of his gifts as an illustrator
is, however, necessary to turn to that memorable array
 drawings by which he was represented in the *Cornhill
'agazine*. In these he had the sort of opportunity that
ited him best, for he was called upon to reproduce the
ncies of skilled story-tellers, and was provided with
aterial that lent itself well to pictorial interpretation.
here were even then inequalities in his work; inequalities,
ɔwever, that could generally be referred to deficiencies in
e suggestion provided by the text with which he had to
:al; but, where the story was of such a nature that it
ıve to the artist a reasonable number of hints, he never
iled to do justice to its picturesque qualities and to
s own artistic ability.

The author with whom he seemed to be most in
·mpathy was Anthony Trollope. The forty-one illustra-

tions executed by him for that novelist's "Orley Farm"
are to be placed in the front rank of his black and white
designs. Trollope, in his autobiography, refers to this story
and its illustrator in the words: "I am fond of 'Orley
Farm,' and I am especially fond of its illustrations by
Millais, which are the best I have seen in any novel in
any language," a sincere opinion that with all its enthusiastic approval can be endorsed almost without reservation.
If Millais did not reach a level of intelligence quite as
remarkable in the drawings for the "Small House at
Allington," "Framley Parsonage," "Phineas Finn," and
in some of his other attempts, at least he never produced
anything that could be criticised as inefficient or wanting in taste, and in execution his work went on year by
year, increasing in power and growing in happy readiness and charm. By the end of the seventies, when he
made himself responsible for the woodcuts in the *edition de
luxe* of Thackeray's "Barry Lyndon," it had gained a degree
of delicacy and refinement, a feeling for beauty of line and
elegance of arrangement, which could hardly be matched.
Whether the Millais of "Barry Lyndon" surpassed the
artist who had handled "Orley Farm" it would be very
difficult to say; but with these two books he certainly
established the standard against which can be measured
not only his own work but that of all other artists in
black and white whom the latter half of this century
has produced.

It would be possible to quote a great many more instances of his success as an illustrator, for during the busiest
period of his production he contributed to a great many
books and magazines ; but it must suffice to call attention
to the real meaning of his intervention in this section of the
work done by the British School. No consideration of
his influence and no review of his performance would be
complete without an appreciative reference to his services
to black and white. As a painter he has a secure place

THE UNMERCIFUL SERVANT

among the chief modern masters of the world ; but what he did for pictorial art was paralleled, if not surpassed, by the victory he won for the draughtsmen, and by his assertion of the dignity and importance of illustration as a form of occupation for even the greatest of art workers.

CHAPTER VIII

COMMENTS AND CRITICISMS

ALTHOUGH it is very much to be questioned whether written criticisms have any particular value as a means of directing the practice of an artist, or as an educational influence affecting his convictions, a degree of historical interest attaches to them, when collected, because they reflect to some extent the unprofessional opinion about his capacities at different periods of his life. They show, if they do nothing else, how his efforts to express himself have been accepted and understood, how his aims have appealed to the people about him, and what has been the effect produced by his manner of asserting the artistic creed, good or bad, to which he has given his adherence. By the tone of these criticisms, indeed, some sort of estimate can be formed of his strength, and of the degree of independence with which he has approached the problems that his profession has presented. If he has never shown any striking individuality, and has been content to jog along comfortably, keeping step with the rest of his fellows, he is probably written down in the records as a most respectable person, with a proper respect for public opinion and a due appreciation of his duty to the community.

But if he has had the courage to take a line of his own, and to think and act for himself independently of any fashion by which the æstheticism of the men about him may have been warped, his treatment by the critics' is sure to have been decidedly violent. What they have set down by way of opinion concerning his work is

LADY MASON

ORLEY FARM

generally virulent enough, and plainly expressive of their resentment at his implied disrespect for the tame beliefs and conventional performances of less active artists. His ideas, as translated by the writers who have taken no trouble to analyse them, are more often than not grossly misrepresented, full of bewildering inconsistencies, and distinguished by neither logic nor sincerity. He is described as a mountebank, a deliberate perverter of the truth, a conspirator striving to undermine established institutions, a man without sense of respect,—as anything, in fact, save an artist with sufficient force of character to wish to do things in the way that he honestly believes to be best.

There always seems to be this sort of proportion maintained between acerbity of criticism and the artistic importance of the man criticised. The stronger the individuality of the worker the more bitter the tone of the remarks made about him, and the more eager the desire to prove him to be unworthy of attention. At first, at all events, he has to put up with the grossest abuse, with attacks that may continue for years. If he is gifted with quite unusual determination and extraordinary firmness of character, he may, by refusing to yield to outcry, live down the opposition, and enjoy in his later career the widest popularity; but if there are any weak places in his armour the onslaught on him may have disastrous results. Many men with exceptional capacities and full of great possibilities have by some small lack of courage been diverted from the course that would have led them to eminence in their profession, and have, in obedience to unreasonable clamour, turned themselves into mere purveyors of the particular commonplaces that the ordinary type of critic makes it his business to advocate.

It was fortunate for the vitality of the British school that Sir John Millais was not a weakling, afraid of hard words and capable of being influenced by noisy assertions. What was the part he played in our art history has been

G

already explained, and it is easy to realise what consequences would have come from any surrender, on his part,
of the principles for which he fought so tenaciously. Yet
if surrender were ever justified by vehemence of opposition
it would have been excusable in his case. Few artists
have had to endure such abuse as that with which he was
bespattered when he began to give the first convincing
proofs of his decision to break away from the mannerism
that he was expected to support. Rarely, indeed, have
critics lost their heads so completely, or shown such
personal animosity to a worker who was certainly not
incapable, and might, if only from a spirit of fairplay, have
been credited with a reasonable amount of sincerity.

As a matter of fact, what was written about Millais,
when he was fighting the battle of living art against the
forces of degenerate ignorance and self-interest, can hardly
be called criticism. It was rather an expression of the
idea, to which many savage tribes pin their faith, that a
loud noise and a threatening attitude will frighten away
an enemy who looks like coming to close quarters. The
device is not particularly logical, and is, as a rule, only
employed when the enemy is numerically weak ; but it
has been known on occasions to serve its purpose, and to
produce a reasonable degree of disorganisation. It is apt
to fail, however, when the oncoming force refuses to play
the game fairly, according to the rules of savage warfare,
and insists upon finding out what amount of solid re-
sistance there may be behind the noise. In such an event
the shouters either decide with amazing promptitude that
their duty calls them at once in another direction, or they
subside engagingly into smiling silence, and do their best
to explain that they have suddenly discovered their
opponents to be a long-lost and ardently-expected band
of brothers.

This was very much what happened in the fifties when
Millais, leading his little party of reformers, appeared

From " Framley Parsonage"   THE CRAWLEY FAMILY

THE BISHOP AND THE KNIGHT

to challenge the great horde of mercenaries that had entrenched itself in the house of art. The shouts were very loud, and the warlike contortions were most terrifying ; but somehow they failed to have any effect. He refused to run away, and with painful determination made evident his intention to fight things out to the bitter end. So in quite a short time it became convenient to admit that he was supporting a good cause, and to substitute adulation for abuse. When once he had clearly proved that he was indifferent to the worst that could be said about him, that he had resolved to work out his own salvation, without help from people who did not appreciate his real purpose, or understand the motives by which he was actuated, everyone was ready to back him up and to gain reflected glory by professions of extreme sympathy with his artistic aims.

The chief weapon that was employed against him, during the period of most persistent and unbalanced attack, was wilful and unscrupulous misrepresentation. The keynote of one type of the arguments used, if they can be dignified by such a term, was struck in the utterance of an inspired critic, who announced that " Pre-Raffleism is a dodge." In the view of the men who wrote after this fashion, Millais had thrown himself into the Pre-Raphaelite movement simply to gain the notoriety that attaches to eccentricity. He wanted to be talked about, to get himself well advertised, and to pose as a kind of æsthetic acrobat, who could attract the gaping wonder of the crowd by his surprising tricks. That he could be sincere in setting himself apart from his contemporaries, was by no means admitted ; it saved trouble to impute to him unworthy motives, and to dismiss him as a discredit to the best traditions of his profession.

Even the writers who took a somewhat higher level, and did not descend to personalities, found, however, a way to suggest that the intention of his art was sinister and

reactionary. "Christ in the House of His Parents," was
an avowal of mediæval superstition, a piece of Romanist
propagandism designed to pervert the morals and upset
the religious convictions of the community. The artist
was a Jesuitical conspirator using his opportunities to
undermine the faith of his countrymen: and all this
because, in accordance with the strictest principles of
Protestantism, he chose to reject a form of æsthetic faith
that seemed to him to have, by a process of inbreeding,
degenerated so grossly that it had ceased to be anything
but a sham. Much more fairly might he have been
attacked for his disregard of all that attractive symbolism
by which the art inspired by the Roman Church is distinguished, for treating a Holy Family with an almost
pagan belief in nature, and an indifference to conventions
that are supposed to have a peculiarly devotional significance. The religious teaching in his picture was not
sweetened with prettiness, nor made palatable by concealing
its serious import under a veil of sensuous beauty; it was
asserted with the stern directness of the grimmest Puritan,
without any concessions to those timid minds that shrink
from plain facts as things with which it is painful to come
in contact.

That his realism did shock a great many people, who
made no attempt to understand its artistic import, becomes
evident enough if the criticisms that deal with the aspect
of his pictures, rather than their symbolism, are compared.
For instance, with reference to "Christ in the House of
His Parents," one critic wrote that "Mr Millais, still
retaining strong marks of that power which distinguished
his Boccacciesque picture last year, has sunk into ex-
travagance bordering in one instance on irreverence";
and another declared that "Mr Millais and his imitators
attempt to engraft themselves on the wildest and most
uncouth productions of the early German School, with a
marked affectation of indifference to everything we are

LAST WORDS

IRENE

accustomed to seek and admire. Mr Millais's principal picture is, to speak plainly, revolting. The attempt to associate the Holy Family with the meanest details of a carpenter's shop with no conceivable omission of misery, of dirt, and even of disease, all finished with the same loathsome minuteness, is disgusting; and, with a surprising power of imitation, this picture serves to show how far mere imitation may fall short, by dryness and conceit, of all dignity and truth."

Quotations of a similar character can be collected in abundance from the papers and magazines published in the spring of 1850. The *Literary Gazette* speaks of the same picture as "a nameless atrocity supposed to represent a verse of Zechariah. A miserable carpenter's shop with two children embracing in the front of the bench, and a naked distorted boy on the right side, are presented to us as high art, in which there is neither taste, drawing, expression, or genius. And yet this style pertains to an imitative school, which, the sooner it is sent back to the dryness and wretched matter-of-fact of old times will be the better. Such things are simply disagreeable, if not worse, and neither can be called the true end of the fine arts."

This writer apparently plumed himself on the possession of a very correct taste, and of a keen judgment as to "the true end of the fine arts." Another seems to have had ideals about the moral mission of the artist, for he gives as his opinion that "Mr Millais, in his picture without a name, which represents a Holy Family in the interior of a carpenter's shop, has been most successful in the least dignified features of his presentment, and in giving to the higher forms, characters, and meanings a circumstantial art-language from which we recoil with loathing and disgust. There are many to whom his work will seem a pictorial blasphemy. Great imitative talents have here been perverted to the use of an eccentricity, both lamentable and revolting"; while a third provides an excellent

specimen of what may be called the sportively personal
style: — "We can hardly imagine anything more ugly,
graceless, and unpleasant, than Mr Millais's picture of
Christ in the carpenter's shop. Such a collection of splay
feet, puffed joints, and mis-shapen limbs was assuredly
never before made within so small a compass. We have
great difficulty in believing a report that this unpleasing
and atrociously affected picture has found a purchaser at a
high price."

From this particular critic came also some remarks about
"Ferdinand lured by Ariel," which was almost as bitterly
disparaged as "Christ in the House of his Parents," and
not less unthinkingly: "Another specimen from the same
brush inspires rather laughter than disgust. A Ferdinand
of most ignoble physiognomy is being lured by a pea-green
monster, intended for Ariel, whilst a row of sprites, such
as it takes a Millais to devise, watch the operation with
turquoise eyes. It would occupy more room than the
thing is worth to expose all the absurdity and impertinence
of this work." The same comparison was made in other
reviews of the pictures of the year. The writer, who considered the picture of the Holy Family a "pictorial
blasphemy," decided that "Ferdinand lured by Ariel" was,
"though better in the painting, yet more senseless in the
conception—a scene built on the contrivances of the stage
manager, but with very bad success"; and yet another,
with an effort to be fair and impartial, found that "the
picture of 'Ariel and Ferdinand' is less offensive in point
of subject and feeling, but scarcely more pardonable in
style. We do not want to see Ariel and the sprites of the
Enchanted Isle in the attitudes and shapes of green goblins,
or the gallant Ferdinand twisted like a posture-master by
Albert Durer. These are mere caprices of genius; but
while we condemn them as deplorable examples of perverted taste, we are not insensible to the power they indicate
over some of the most curious spells of art."

From "The Small House at Allington"

THE BOARD

Presumably the whole of these noisy misinterpreters of the artist's intentions took their cue from the *Times*, as the chief disseminator of journalistic opinion. They were certainly egged on by it to do their worst, and encouraged in any exaggerated courses they might like to adopt. The *Times*, when it declared that "that morbid infatuation which sacrifices truth, beauty, and genuine feeling, to mere eccentricity, deserves no quarter at the hands of the public," simply pilloried the lad of twenty and invited every passer-by to throw mud at him. No wonder Millais spoke, in after years, of the fifties as the time when he was "so dreadfully bullied"; he must, for all his astonishing self-reliance and firmness of faith in the absolute justice of his cause, very often have found it difficult to stand against the storm.

It is, however, likely that he saw through the bluster and violence of the attacks upon him, and was induced to hold on by a consciousness that more than half of the vehemence of his opponents arose from their real fear of his ability. If he had been less of a menace to the order of things that existed in the art world when he was a boy, he would not have been held to be worth so much trouble. The desire to crush him arose from the knowledge that his influence, if allowed to develop, would become irresistible; he was too distinct a personality to remain of no account in art politics when once he had gained a hearing, and the only chance was to nip his independence in the bud. Even if he had but a partial appreciation of the uneasiness that he was creating among the men who were straining every nerve to keep their popularity, he must have felt that there was hope of eventual victory, hope enough to justify him in doggedly resisting every effort to drive him from the position he had taken up.

What this position was, and why it was assailed so furiously, even by the critics who had judgment enough to recognise the greatness of the natural gifts with which

Millais was endowed, is very well explained in an article on the Pre-Raphaelite faith that Mr F. G. Stephens, who could write with full authority on the subject, contributed to the *London Review* in 1862—so well explained, indeed, that one of the most significant passages is worth quoting verbatim : " If students referred to the productions of those artists who differed from themselves only in being of greater age, and servilely adopted the dogmas and practice of their seniors, without any reference to nature, such a practice, the Brotherhood averred, could not but produce a school of painters, each generation of whom would be more effete, because more conventionalised, than that which preceded it, and to whose experience they looked for guidance.

"The end of this might be guessed, said the Pre-Raphaelite Brotherhood in the flush of youthful confidence, and they even dared to add that the result of following such a pernicious system was obvious in the works of almost every one of their own contemporaries, and in those produced by their immediate forerunners. Declaring that the followers of Raphael had ruined the art, simply because they were followers of Raphael, and not humble students of nature, and reflecting, not without bitterness, upon the practice of the Prince of Painters himself when he condescended to serve a vile Court, the Pre-Raphaelite Brotherhood, with characteristic audacity, and with a seriousness which was half veiled in the fantastic assumption of their Society's peculiar title, determined that their own works should show a different motive in art, and that they themselves, with all the powers and skill that were within them, would, whatever the consequences might be, pursue a practice widely removed from that of those whom they and all the world about them had been taught to respect or imitate.

"Half in fun, the Brotherhood called itself 'Pre-Raphaelite,' adopting that title rather to express a full measure of admiration for the motive which guided the

ON THE WATER

From "Once a Week"

great painters preceding Raphael than intending it to be understood, as the critics of a dozen years ago received it, as chosen in approbation of the oftentimes fantastic, more often ascetic, and almost invariably imperfect systems of execution to which the undeveloped powers of painting possessed by the early Italian artists limited so cruelly their achievements on the panel or the convent wall. Considering how small were the attainments demanded of the art critics of the time in question, it is not surprising they should have fallen into this absurdity. Few of these men knew enough of the history of the art they abused the public mind about, to be able to recognise the real state of the case, still less were they prepared to comprehend the true qualities which shine through the most bizarre failures of execution, most of them the result of over-earnestness and a devout desire to do right, which beset the artists they ridiculed.

"Indulgence for youth of their own day, an enlightened and foreseeing regard to the importance of that which lay behind the most audacious declarations of the Brotherhood, were not to be expected from such men. A few only saw that something might come out of an idea so boldly enunciated, and, notwithstanding the vivid colours of its ridiculous side, sufficiently well expressed to have merited a gentler consideration than it received."

How correct was this estimate of the so-called critical opinion of the early fifties, is excellently proved by the remarks with which the *Times* accompanied its demand that no quarter should be given to Millais and his friends. With reference to his "Mariana" it declared that, "these young artists have unfortunately become notorious by addicting themselves to an antiquated style and an affected simplicity in painting. . . . We can extend no toleration to a mere senile imitation of the cramped style, false perspective, and crude colour of remote antiquity. We want not to see what Fuseli termed drapery ' snapped

instead of folded,' faces bloated into apoplexy, or ex-
tenuated skeletons; colour borrowed from the jars in
a druggist's shop, and expression forced into caricature."
It was this criticism particularly that aroused Mr Ruskin
into his active championship of the Pre-Raphaelites, and
drew from him that famous letter to the *Times* in which
he exposed the fallacies of the newspaper arguments.
He disposed bit by bit of the charges of technical incompetence which were arrayed against the young artists,
defending their knowledge of perspective, praising their
painting, and directly contradicting the reference to
Fuseli by the assertion that "there is not a single
study of drapery in the whole Academy, be it in large
works or small, which, for perfect truth, power, and finish,
could be compared, for an instant, with the white draperies
on the table of Mr Millais's ' Mariana,' and of the right-
hand figure in the same painter's ' Dove returning to the
Ark.'"

Although this powerful support, from a man who was
prepared to fight with all his energies on the side of the
Brotherhood, did not fail in its ultimate effect, the chorus
of abuse ceased only when it became evident that the
public sympathised with the artists and not with the
critics who found fault with them.   Because Millais was
the most prominent, the most conspicuously talented
member of the group, he was fixed upon as the chief
and most dangerous figure in a movement that had to
be checked at all costs.   As he towered over the rest,
he was chosen as the target for the missiles, that the men
of "small attainments" hurled at Pre-Raphaelitism ; and,
for the same reason, when the cause for which he was
striving had won its way to acceptance, he received the
fullest share of the adulation that is always lavished
upon success.   ˙

Anything like unanimity of praise was, however, a long
time coming.   It was necessarily a slow growth, and took

THE MONK

From "Once a Week"

MARGARET WILSON
THE SCOTTISH MARTYR

many years in development. But a constantly increasing tendency to judge him more fairly appeared among the newer men, who, with better balanced judgment, refused to adopt the gross exaggerations of the old type of criticism. Year by year the dilution of the blind and thoughtless invective with serious and rational consideration became more perceptible, and with each successive picture he was, it could be seen, making more secure his hold upon educated taste. " The Order of Release," for instance, which was at first generally assailed, because its marvellous realism was unappreciated, drew later on from Mr Andrew Lang an expression of the opinion that "the stamp of actual truth is on it, and if ever such an event happened, if ever a Highlander's wife brought a pardon for her husband to a reluctant turnkey, things must have occurred thus. The work is saved by expression and colour from the realism of a photograph. . . . The subject and the sentiment, no less than the treatment, made this picture a complete success." And of " The Rescue," a ' very great " work, according to Mr Ruskin, another critic wrote: "Apart from the rapture of the mother, the intense gladness of one of the children's faces as she embraces the lady's neck, and the self-restrained, yet frightened, looks of the boy, who clings about the shoulders of the deliverer, are enough to immortalise the picture and its painter."

In these comments are seen the first fruits of his victory, the earliest signs of that enthusiastic approval which he enjoyed in ample measure for the latter part of his life. A few quotations from the opinions of the men who have been able to place his pictures of many periods in their right relation, and to estimate the full value and significance of the changes in his manner and methods, will serve to establish a complete comparison between the criticism that was intended to crush him and that which recorded his success. Sir Walter Armstrong,

in the biography which he wrote in 1886, as a special
number of the *Art Journal*, says: "In our living school
of English painters, Sir John Everett Millais enjoys by
far the widest fame; for thirty-five years the public has
concerned itself with his work, and for more than a quarter
of a century, from the year of the 'Black Brunswicker'
downwards, no contributions to the Academy have excited so much interest as his. Beginning as a *préraphaélite
enragé*, he promises to end a true successor of Gainsborough and Reynolds; and through the whole of his
transmutations, or rather of his development — for, after
all, the progress from the 'Isabella' of 1849 to the 'Lady
Peggy Primrose' of 1885 is but the growth of four
centuries writ small on a single brow—he has at once
preserved his own rather militant sincerity, and carried
his public with him."

Mr M. H. Spielmann, in his "In Memoriam" notice, that
appeared in the *Magazine of Art* for September 1896,
declares that "now not England only, but with her the
whole wide world of art, mourns her greatest painter of
the century, the most universally beloved man who,
through his genius, has ever made his way into the
heart and the affections of a nation. . . . A life of glory
prematurely cut short, has been snatched away, leaving
English art deprived of its brightest, if not its greatest
ornament"; and in his book dealing with the memorial
exhibition at the Academy in 1898, is this passage
"Standing amid this series of fine achievements, among
which are not a few indisputable masterpieces, one may
well recall the words that Millais spoke before the Royal
Academy Commission in 1864, when he championed the
candidature of such men as John Leech as members of
that body: 'Very few of us painters will leave behind
us such good and valuable work as he has left. You
will never find a bit of false sentiment in anything he
did.' The work with which Millais has endowed his

From "Sister Anna's Probation"   ANNA AND HER LOVER

THE PLAGUE OF ELLIANT

From "Once a Week"

ə's labour which he has left behind, will
ι thrill of gratitude and pride through the
 man who, caring for his country's fame,
ıd on this great collection, unprecedented
:rits in modern times, and has recognised
can be said that the 'false sentiment' he
ts any one of them.   The main cause for
:he poorer pictures, seen together, make a
:r than they did when they were seen by
ıe successes are so brilliant, that the inferior
ıally to gain in the effulgence of the best.
ıame of Millais stood higher than it does
is genius is spread out before us, and his
ven in the power of his art."
ok, Professor Muther's "History of Modern
. is important because it represents Contin-
ıut the artist's work, he is spoken of as "one
 the history of nineteenth-century painting
ible and healthy as they are many-sided.
ɔne who could have developed so swiftly
 the most minute exactness to one of the
ɔreadth; not óne who could have united
:onception with such an enormous know-
beings; not one who could have been so
 variety—at one moment charming, at
, at another entirely positive"; and else-
.me book it is remarked that, "this same
:r of character commands the soft, light
ɛr of children as few others.   No one since
Gainsborough has painted with so much
:illais the dazzling freshness of English
getic pose of a boy's head or the beauty
girl—a thing which stands in the world
ıe had triumphed, that he had silenced
 secured that crown of thoughtful and
·obation for which every artist strives,

these tributes to his power declare with all possible emphasis. To multiply such quotations would be easy enough; the applause that he received at last was unstinted, and without a discordant note, but it was honest, and it expressed the true conviction of people who knew him well and loved him because they did know him.

It was characteristic of his eager and straightforward nature that he should derive from his success the most hearty enjoyment. Conceit he had none; but he delighted in the consciousness that his youthful indifference to clamour, and his sturdy refusal to bend to the storm that raged so furiously about him then, should have been in the end justified publicly and openly. He rejoiced to think that the labours of his life had not been wasted, and that he had helped to give to the art of this country a renewed vitality that promises now to remain to it permanently.

What he felt about his work is expressed truly in Mr Spielmann's book: "It is well that the country should appreciate the triumph achieved in this great exhibition at Burlington House — that triumph to which, stretched on his death-bed, the great painter looked forward with such keen eagerness and passionate interest, a glory not for himself alone, but shared, by his favour, by the whole English School. He knew that it would 'vindicate' him and lying under the stern verdict of fate, he found consolation in the thought; not from vanity, but from love o his art. And if the world will regard it aright, it wil perceive that this collection of the greater part of Millais' life-work, now gathered on the scene of his early struggle and subsequent victory, constitutes the most importan purely artistic event of the kind that has taken place ii the present century. Just as the cycle is drawing to it close, the public has the good fortune of witnessing display of brilliancy, virile power, force, variety of ex pression, technical ability, and intuitive 'rightness' whic assuredly none of us will ever see again from the hand (

one man." It was a vindication on which any artist might justifiably have prided himself, and there is no difficulty in believing that to Sir John Millais the knowledge that it would be made so completely must have been peculiarly gratifying.

There is one other point to note, because it marks beyond dispute the growth of his reputation through the half-century covered by his working life, and that is the ever-increasing anxiety of collectors to become possessed of his pictures. The prices that his canvases would fetch in his later years compared strangely with the £250 that was thought to be a great sum for anyone to give for "Christ in the House of His Parents," or with the £150, that was paid to him in instalments of £50, for "The Huguenot"; and since his death he has, by the verdict of the sale-room, been accorded a place among the old masters. The Chantrey Fund Trustees acquired, for £2000, "Speak! Speak!" in 1895 ; and, some years before, his "Vale of Rest," for which, when it was first exhibited, no one would pay the price, £600, put upon it, had brought, when the Graham collection was dispersed, 3000 guineas. For "The Order of Release" he received £400 in 1853; by 1879 it had reached £2835, and in 1898 it was sold for 5000 guineas. The "Black Brunswicker" rose from £819 in 1862, to £2782 in 1898 ; and in the same year "Afternoon Tea" was sold for £1365, and "Yes" for £1050. "The Proscribed Royalist" brought £551 in 1862, and £2100 in 1897 ; and in the present year 4500 guineas were paid at Christie's for "The Minuet."

These may fairly be classed as comments on his career. The money value of a work of art does not necessarily bear any relation to its æsthetic worth, but keen competition between men of means for the privilege of possessing the canvases of any particular artist is, at all events, a proof that he is recognised as a leader in the art world, and a prominent figure among his contemporaries. That this sign of appreciation was accorded to Sir John Millais in his lifetime was a fair compensation for his early struggles. He had fought a good fight, and wealth and honours came to him happily in full measure, while he was yet young enough to enjoy them to the utmost. His, at least, was not the fate that has befallen so many other great workers in art, to suffer poverty and unhappiness through long years of labour, sustained only by the conviction that posterity would do justice to his memory

From " Home Affections "

THERE IS NAE LUCK
ABOUT THE HOUSE

CHRONOLOGICAL LIST OF PAINTINGS

*This List is reprinted by the kind permission of Mr M. H. Spielmann, from
is book entitled " Millais and His Works." The dates given are those at
hich, as nearly as can be ascertained, the various works were completed.*

1841

UPID CROWNED WITH FLOWERS

c. 1845

*ILLIAM HUGH FENN (destroyed
  picture)

1846

APTISM OF GUTHREN THE DANE
IZARRO SEIZING THE INCA OF PERU
HE MOORISH CHIEF

1847

HE TRIBE OF BENJAMIN SEIZING
  THE DAUGHTERS OF SHILOH
LGIVA
HE WIDOW'S MITE
TUDY OF AN INDIAN'S HEAD
HILDHOOD ⎫
OUTH   ⎪
IANHOOD ⎬ (Panels for the
GE   ⎪   Judges' Lodgings
IUSIC   ⎪   at Leeds)
RT   ⎭
YMON (study for Cymon and
  Iphigenia)

1848

*. HUGH FENN
OMEO AND JULIET (last scene)

1849

ABELLA (Lorenzo and Isabella)
ORTRAIT OF A GENTLEMAN AND
  HIS GRANDCHILD (Mr Wyatt)
ERDINAND LURED BY ARIEL
HRIST IN THE HOUSE OF HIS
  PARENTS

1850

HOMAS COMBE
HE WOODMAN'S DAUGHTER

1851

CYMON AND IPHIGENIA
MARIANA IN THE MOATED GRANGE
RETURN OF THE DOVE TO THE ARK
  OR "DAUGHTERS OF NOAH CAR-
  ESSING THE DOVE, ETC."; OR
  "WIVES OF THE SONS OF NOAH"
THE BRIDESMAID ("ALL HALLOW'S
  E'EN ")

1852

MEMORY
OPHELIA
THE HUGUENOT
THE HUGUENOT (Sketch)
THE HUGUENOT (Study)
MRS COVENTRY K. PATMORE
HEAD OF OPHELIA (with Wreath)

1853

THE ORDER OF RELEASE
THE PROSCRIBED ROYALIST, 1651
THE PROSCRIBED ROYALIST
ST GEORGE AND THE DRAGON (sign-
  board)

1854

WAITING (or A Girl at a Stile)
A HIGHLAND LASSIE (or Head of a
  Scotch Girl)
JOHN RUSKIN
LANDSCAPE STUDY OF WATERFALL
MISS SIDDAL

1855

THE RESCUE
THE RANDOM SHOT (originally
  " L'Enfant du Régiment ")

1856

THE CONCLUSION OF PEACE, 1856
  (correct title " Peace Concluded ")

H

113

AUTUMN LEAVES
THE BLIND GIRL
"PORTRAIT OF A GENTLEMAN" (or
    "The Picture-book")
POT POURRI

1857

HEAD OF A GIRL
HEAD OF A GIRL
SIR ISUMBRAS AT THE FORD ("A
    Dream of the Past")
THE ESCAPE OF A HERETIC, 1559
THE ESCAPE OF A HERETIC, 1559
    (small oil version)
NEWS FROM HOME
WEDDING CARDS

1858

THE VALE OF REST

1859

THE LOVE OF JAMES I. OF SCOT-
    LAND
APPLE-BLOSSOMS ("Spring")
CHILDREN GATHERING GRAPES
HEAD OF A LADY (cutting a lock of
    hair)
MEDITATION
HEAD OF A WOMAN

1860

THE BLACK BRUNSWICKER
THE RIVALS

1861

THE RINGLET (see 1859)

1862

THE RANSOM
THE WHITE COCKADE
MRS CHARLES FREEMAN
"TRUST ME!"
PARABLE OF THE LOST PIECE OF
    MONEY
THE BRIDE
LADY IN A GARDEN
A PASTORAL
HEAD OF A GIRL
WANDERING THOUGHTS
THE MUSIC MISTRESS

1863

MY FIRST SERMON
MY SECOND SERMON

THE EVE OF ST AGNES
THE EVE OF ST AGNES (small ve-
    sion)
THE EVE OF ST AGNES (small ve
    sion)
THE EVE OF ST AGNES (oil sketch
HENRY MANNERS (MARQUESS (
    GRANBY)
SUSPENSE
THE WOLF'S DEN
BRIDESMAID THROWING THE LUCK
    SLIPPER

1864

LEISURE HOURS
"CHARLIE IS MY DARLING"
"SWALLOW! SWALLOW!"
MASTER WYCLIF TAYLOR (son (
    Mr Tom Taylor)
LILY (daughter of J. Noble, Esq.)
HAROLD (son of the Dowager-Coun
    tess of Winchelsea)
THE CONJUROR
RED RIDING HOOD

1865

THE PARABLE OF THE TARES (c
    the Enemy sowing Tares)
JOAN OF ARC
ESTHER
THE ROMANS LEAVING BRITAIN
THE GREEK SLAVE
ATTENTION DIVERTED

1866

THE MINUET

1867

ASLEEP (correct title "SLEEPING")
JUST AWAKE (correct title "WAK-
    ING")
JEPHTHAH
MASTER CAYLEY

1868

STELLA
VANESSA
SIR JOHN FOWLER, BART., C.E.
ROSALIND AND CELIA
A SOUVENIR OF VELASQUEZ
SISTERS
GREENWICH PENSIONERS AT THE
    TOMB OF NELSON (originally
    "Pilgrims to St Paul's")

GREENWICH PENSIONERS AT THE TOMB OF NELSON (small oil version)
THE BRIDE
HEAD OF A GIRL
EXCELSIOR
MILKING TIME

THE NORTH-WEST PASSAGE
THE FRINGE OF THE MOOR
MISS EVELEEN TENNANT (Mrs F. H. Myers)
STILL FOR A MOMENT
A DAY-DREAM

1869

THE GAMBLER'S WIFE
NINA, DAUGHTER OF F. LEHMANN, ESQ.
A DREAM OF DAWN
THE END OF THE CHAPTER

1870

A WIDOW'S MITE
A FLOOD
CHILL OCTOBER
THE BOYHOOD OF RALEIGH
SIR JOHN KELK, BART.
THE KNIGHT ERRANT
MARCHIONESS OF HUNTLY
THE MARTYR OF THE SOLWAY

1871

"YES OR NO?"
FLOWING TO THE RIVER
GEORGE GROTE
"VICTORY, O LORD!"
A SOMNAMBULIST

1872

MRS HEUGH
"HEARTS ARE TRUMPS"
SIR JAMES PAGET
FLOWING TO THE SEA
MASTER LIDDELL
MARQUESS OF WESTMINSTER
"OH! THAT A DREAM SO LONG ENJOYED, ETC."

1873

HON. WALTER ROTHSCHILD
EARLY DAYS
SCOTCH FIRS
MRS BISCHOFFSHEIM
NEW LAID EGGS
SIR WILLIAM STERNDALE BENNETT
WINTER FUEL

1874

THE PICTURE OF HEALTH

1875

FORBIDDEN FRUIT
EVELINE, DAUGHTER OF T. EVANS LEES, ESQ.
GRACIA, DAUGHTER OF T. EVANS LEES, ESQ.
"NO!"
THE DESERTED GARDEN
"OVER THE HILLS AND FAR AWAY"
"MODEL," A BASSET HOUND
THE CONVALESCENT
THE CROWN OF LOVE

1876

"STITCH! STITCH! STITCH!"
MRS SEBASTIAN SCHLESINGER
A YEOMAN OF THE GUARD
TWIN DAUGHTERS OF T. R. HOARE, ESQ. ("Twins")
GETTING BETTER
GEORGE MILLAIS
EVERETT MILLAIS
MISS EFFIE MILLAIS
MISS MARY MILLAIS
MISS ALICE CAROLINE MILLAIS
ITALIAN GIRL, AN (for a time known as "Pippa")
LORD LYTTON
DUCHESS OF WESTMINSTER
COUNTESS GROSVENOR
LADY BEATRICE GROSVENOR
LORD RONALD GOWER
THE SOUND OF MANY WATERS

1877

THE EARL OF SHAFTESBURY
EFFIE DEANS
A GOOD RESOLVE
"YES!"
PUSS-IN-BOOTS
BRIGHT EYES
MARCHIONESS OF ORMONDE
THOMAS CARLYLE

1878

MRS STIBBARD
A JERSEY LILY
THE PRINCES IN THE TOWER
ST MARTIN'S SUMMER
COUNTESS OF CARYSFORT
BRIDE OF LAMMERMOOR

1879

MISS HERMIONE SCHENLEY
THE BRIDESMAID
MRS JOPLING
MRS S. H. BEDDINGTON
RT. HON. W. E. GLADSTONE
THE PRINCESS ELIZABETH
MISS BEATRICE CAIRD
CHERRY RIPE
URQUHART CASTLE
MRS ARTHUR KENNARD
MISS CATHERINE MURIEL COWELL
  STEPNEY (originally " Portrait of
  a Child ")

1880

BISHOP FRASER
MRS PERUGINI
DIANA VERNON
RT. HON. JOHN BRIGHT
MRS CAIRD
" CUCKOO "
LUTHER HOLDEN, P.R.C.S.
MISS EVELYN OTWAY
SIR JOHN E. MILLAIS, BART.
GIRL WITH VIOLETS (small picture)
GIRL AT THE STILE (small picture)
SIR GILBERT GREENALL

1881

D. THWAITES
CARDINAL NEWMAN
CHILDREN OF OCTAVIUS MOULTON
  BARRETT, ESQ.
" SWEETEST EYES WERE EVER
  SEEN "
REV. JOHN CAIRD, D.D.
SIR J. D. ASTLEY, BART.
ALFRED, LORD TENNYSON
SIR HENRY THOMPSON
LITTLE MRS GAMP
CINDERELLA
CAPTAIN JAMES (Royal Scots Greys)
MRS JAMES (Miss Effie Millais)
CALLER HERRIN'

DUCHESS OF WESTMINSTER (Lady
  Constance Leveson-Gower)
LORD WIMBORNE
THE EARL OF BEACONSFIELD
NON ANGLI SED ANGELI

1882

POMONA
MRS JAMES STERN
OLIVIA
DUCHESS OF WESTMINSTER
" FOR THE SQUIRE "
J. C. HOOK, R.A.
H.R.H. THE PRINCESS MARIE OF
  EDINBURGH ("A Little Duchess")
THE STOWAWAY
NELL GWYNNE (begun by Land-
  seer and completed by Millais)
DOROTHY THORPE
MRS RICHARD BUDGETT
MRS GARROW-WHITBY
LOVE BIRDS (originally " Une
  Grande Dame ")
THE CAPTIVE
DROPPED FROM THE NEST

1883

MARQUESS OF SALISBURY
FORGET-ME-NOT
THE GREY LADY
T. H. ISMAY
CHARLES WARING
MASTER FREEMAN
SIR JOHN E. MILLAIS, BART., P.R.

1884

LITTLE MISS MUFFETT
PERFECT BLISS
AN IDYLL, 1745
LADY PEGGY PRIMROSE
LADY CAMPBELL
A MESSAGE FROM THE SEA
THE MISTLETOE-GATHERER
SIR HENRY IRVING
FLEETWOOD WILSON
LADY GILBERT GREENALL
MISS SCOTT (of Philadelphia)
MARQUESS OF LORNE

1885

THE RULING PASSION (or "The
  Ornithologist ")
ORPHANS

A WAIF
SIMON FRASER
FOUND (landscape and figures in the picture by Landseer)
MISS MARGARET MILLAIS
RT. HON. W. E. GLADSTONE

1886

LILACS
BUBBLES
T. O. BARLOW, R.A.
RUDDIER THAN THE CHERRY
LORD ESHER
PORTIA
MERCY ! ST BARTHOLOMEW'S DAY, 1572

1887

MRS CHARLES STUART WORTLEY
THE NEST
MURTHLY MOSS, PERTHSHIRE
PENSEROSO
ALLEGRO
EARL OF ROSEBERY
MARQUESS OF HARTINGTON
CLARISSA

1888

MRS PAUL HARDY
THE LAST ROSE OF SUMMER
MURTHLY WATER
THE OLD GARDEN
C. J. WERTHEIMER
CHRISTMAS EVE
TWA BAIRNS (Frederick and Mary Stewart Phillips, children of Frederick Phillips, Esq. of Godshill, Isle of Wight)
SIR ARTHUR SULLIVAN
FORLORN

1889

SHELLING PEAS
DUCKLINGS
AFTERNOON TEA (called by the artist "Gossips")

1890

DEW DRENCHED FURZE
LINGERING AUTUMN
"THE MOON IS UP AND YET IT IS NOT NIGHT"
RT. HON. W. E. GLADSTONE, M.P., AND HIS GRANDSON
PORTRAIT OF A LADY
MASTER RANKEN

1891

HON. MRS HERBERT GIBBS
GLEN BIRNAM
GRACE
MRS JOSEPH CHAMBERLAIN
MRS CHARLES WERTHEIMER
DOROTHY, DAUGHTER OF MRS HARRY LAWSON

1892

"THE LITTLE SPEEDWELL'S DARLING BLUE"
"BLOW, BLOW, THOU WINTER WIND !"
HALCYON WEATHER
MASTER ANTHONY DE ROTHSCHILD
"SWEET EMMA MORELAND"

1893

JOHN HARE
THE GIRLHOOD OF ST THERESA
PENSIVE (or Sad)
MERRY

1895

"SPEAK ! SPEAK !"
TIME THE REAPER
ST STEPHEN
THE EMPTY CAGE
ADA, DAUGHTER OF ROBERT RINTOUL SIMON, ESQ.
A DISCIPLE

1895

A FORERUNNER
SIR ROBERT PULLAR
SIR RICHARD QUAIN, BART.
STANLEY LEIGHTON, M.P.
THE HON. JOHN NEVILLE MANNERS
THE MARCHIONESS OF TWEEDDALE
J. G. MILLAIS (unfinished)

Dates Uncertain

BRIDE, THE
BRIGHT EYES
COLLINS, WILKIE
DIGGING OUT THE OTTER IN THE VALLEY OF THE TAY. (Landscape, sky, and figures by Millais)
DU MAURIER, GEORGE
GOOD KNIGHT, THE
HUNT, W.
SCHOOL TEACHER, THE
WINTER GARDEN

INDEX

This Index does not include the pictures given in the Chronological List
pp. 113-117.

I

www.ingramcontent.com/pod-product-compliance
Lightning Source LLC
Chambersburg PA
CBHW060600030726
47498CB00005B/1473